His hand shot up and caught hers.

All Lauren was aware of was the feel of his skin. Familiar. Addictive. Her heart started racing in her chest as though her body suddenly remembered his touch. Flashes of their nights together rushed to her mind all at once.

And just like that, their chemistry was back in full force. Like a lightning bolt had struck them. She wasn't sure what had changed, but things were definitely different today.

He noticed it, too. His green eyes narrowed. There was a knowing heat in his gaze. It was enough to make her cheeks flame with embarrassment, and this time she had no mask to hide it.

"You're not very good at hiding what you're thinking. Your face is very expressive. I like being able to see your whole face. I feel like with your mask on I was missing out on so many facets of your emotions."

* * *

Billionaire Behind the Mask
by Andrea Laurence is part of the
Texas Cattleman's Club: Rags to Riches series.

Dear Reader,

I don't do many Texas Cattleman's Club books. In fact, this is only my second one out of over thirty Harlequin Desire titles. Alpha cowboys are amazing, but my heroes always lean toward clean-cut playboys with smart mouths—better suited for the boardroom than the open range. But every now and then, a hero pops up in the TCC universe that's made for me. This is one of those stories. A fish out of water, a masquerade ball and a pair of rich, sexy twins...yes, please!

Lauren's story is truly a Cinderella tale, complete with a fairy godmother/stylist to provide her a dress and a ride to the ball. Her world is her kitchen and her food, so stepping out that night in a red gown and falling into the arms of Sutton's big, bad wolf is unexpected...and exhilarating. And proof that the right dress and shoes (however uncomfortable they might be) can change your life. It was a fun ride to write and, hopefully, it will be just as much fun to read.

If you enjoyed Sutton and Lauren's story, tell me by visiting my website at www.andrealaurence.com, like my fan page on Facebook (authorandrealaurence), or follow me on Twitter (andrea_laurence), Instagram (aclaurence) and BookBub (andrea-laurence). I'd love to hear from you!

Enjoy,

Andrea

ANDREA LAURENCE

BILLIONAIRE BEHIND THE MASK

HARLEQUIN
DESIRE

Special thanks and acknowledgment are given to Andrea Laurence for her contribution to the Texas Cattleman's Club: Rags to Riches miniseries.

HARLEQUIN®
DESIRE™

ISBN-13: 978-1-335-20937-5

Billionaire Behind the Mask

This edition published by arrangement with Harlequin Books S.A.

For questions and comments about the quality of this book, please contact us at CustomerService@Harlequin.com.

Harlequin Enterprises ULC
22 Adelaide St. West, 40th Floor
Toronto, Ontario M5H 4E3, Canada
www.Harlequin.com

Printed in U.S.A.

Andrea Laurence is an award-winning contemporary author who has been a lover of books and writing stories since she learned to read. A dedicated West Coast girl transplanted into the Deep South, she's constantly trying to develop a taste for sweet tea and grits while caring for her boyfriend and an old bulldog. You can contact Andrea at her website: www.andrealaurence.com.

Books by Andrea Laurence

Harlequin Desire

Millionaires of Manhattan

What Lies Beneath
More Than He Expected
His Lover's Little Secret
The CEO's Unexpected Child
Little Secrets: Secretly Pregnant
Rags to Riches Baby
One Unforgettable Weekend
The Boyfriend Arrangement

Switched!

From Mistake to Millions
From Riches to Redemption
From Seduction to Secrets

Texas Cattleman's Club: Rags to Riches

Billionaire Behind the Mask

Visit her Author Profile page at Harlequin.com, or andrealaurence.com, for more titles.

You can also find Andrea Laurence on Facebook, along with other Harlequin Desire authors, at www.Facebook.com/harlequindesireauthors!

To Senior Editor Extraordinaire Stacy Boyd
& My Fellow TCC Authors:

It's been a pleasure, as always,
to create with you.

One

This was a bad idea, but no one seemed to realize it but Lauren.

Everyone else in her life was thrilled that she'd won the local radio contest that awarded her a glamorous makeover, limo transportation and tickets for two to the charity masquerade ball at the Texas Cattleman's Club. She was less excited by the news because, in all honesty, Lauren Roberts was not the kind of person to enter a contest like that. It was even called the *Cinderella Sweepstakes*. How over the top was that? Like she was going to meet her Prince Charming out on the dance floor or something. The last time she'd stepped foot in this building, it had been a nightmare, not a dream come true.

No, she had no interest in going to that party or hanging out with those people at the club. Unfortunately, she'd been entered by her well-meaning friend and employee Amy without her knowledge. The next thing she knew, she was spending a normally lucrative Saturday at a day spa. She should've been with one of her food trucks downtown. She was *always* at one of her food trucks, but she supposed that was the point Amy was trying to make by entering her in the contest.

So, she had no social life. It didn't bother her. She had two successful food trucks and a booming career as a chef. That was more important to her. Spending a day getting steam facials, manicures and highlights in her hair was a waste of time and money to Lauren. In her day-to-day life, none of that mattered. Her dark brown hair was always back in a bun, where no one would see the caramel highlights that were added. She got plenty of steam facials from the hot water trays in the trucks that kept food warm. And no one would see pretty nails when she was wearing food service gloves.

The whole thing was preposterous, but in the end she'd agreed to go. Because, like it or not, if she wanted to get a permanent location in Royal, Texas, and build a high-end clientele, she needed to spend more time with the kind of people that frequented the club. With that in mind, she'd put on the bright red dress that was chosen for her by the personal shopper for the contest, tied on her mask and hoped for the best.

Everyone had told her to enjoy herself. Have fun. Make the most of her night off without worrying about whether one of the trucks ran out of supplies or if Javier, the line cook, made the nightly deposit. Amy had things under control, but letting go was hard to do. It would require some alcohol. But she could do it. And deep down, Lauren knew she *needed* to do it.

This wasn't high school anymore. She could go to this party and have a good time. With the ornate mask she was wearing, she could even pretend to be someone else tonight. No one would expect mousy, workaholic chef Lauren Roberts to be at the club anyway. She didn't belong here. But the mysterious woman in red—she *could* fit in…and have an amazing time this evening.

She just had to get out of the damn limo.

The driver had been standing patiently with the door open for quite a while now, waiting for Lauren to step out. At this point, she was probably causing a traffic jam.

"Ma'am?" he asked at last, with concern lining his face.

"Yes, sorry." Lauren snatched up her black, beaded clutch and forced herself out of the limousine. She took a step up the stairs to the grand entrance and stopped again. It looked very different from what she remembered, but it had been eleven years since she'd been to the club. While appearances had changed both for her and the building itself, the feelings it roused in her were the same: excitement followed quickly by anxiety and a touch of dread.

She turned to see if her getaway car was still available, but the driver and the limo were down the road already. Another car had pulled up and was unloading a crowd of people that would swallow her up if she didn't move. Nowhere to go but forward to face her fears.

Lauren lifted the hem of her slinky red gown and climbed the steps to the entrance. At the door, a table was set up to collect tickets for the event.

"Tickets, ma'am?" the man sitting at the table asked. He was wearing a tuxedo with a Guy Fawkes mask.

"My name should be on the list," she replied. "Lauren Roberts?"

He checked a paper he had beside him. "It's showing it's for a party of two. Are you expecting a guest?"

"No, it's just me tonight." Although she'd won two tickets, her personal life was so nonexistent she couldn't scrape together a date in time for the party. She should've just brought Amy, but she knew she would have clung to her best friend all night. Lauren sighed. If she was going to make the most of tonight, she needed to get out of her comfort zone and talk to strangers.

"All the better for the single gentlemen here tonight," the man said.

Lauren couldn't see his expression behind his mask to see if he was joking. He sounded completely serious. The makeover must've worked wonders. Normally, she was completely under the radar of most men in this town. Invisible. Could highlights and a glamorous dress make that big of a difference?

"I'll see you in there later, Miss Roberts."

She wished her mask covered her whole face so he couldn't see the awkward blush that was no doubt creeping up beneath her foundation. "Thank you," she stammered and rushed past him into the club when no other valid response came to mind.

As she stepped through the doorway, the sound of music, laughter and voices called to her. She went down the hall, passing the office and the daycare center she didn't remember being there before, and then stopped short as it opened up into the main room.

It was a lot like the last time she'd come. Dark lighting, loud music, a sea of bodies on the dance floor and loitering around the edges of the room. The difference was that these weren't teenagers at a dance. They were adults. Rich ones. The kind that could invest in her restaurant, or at the very least become patrons someday. They weren't going to play cruel pranks or laugh at her. They were just having a good time and raising money for charity. She needed to just blend in and have a good time, too.

The last thought propelled her forward.

"May I take your coat?" a younger girl asked as she manned the coat check.

Lauren slipped out of her leather jacket and handed it over. It didn't exactly go with the red, beaded gown anyway, but October had brought an unexpected chill to the air. It was early for Texas, but she'd take it. Fall was her favorite time of year. She got to experiment with new seasonal flavors on the truck menus, find a pumpkin patch to explore, hand out candy to trick-or-treaters…and she wasn't dying from the heat in the trucks each day.

She wanted a permanent storefront for her restaurant, even if just for the air-conditioning. When she was parked at a location, a generator would run some things, but not air. In the summer, that meant hot food, steamy trays and no respite from the heat, short of sticking her head in the refrigerator.

She took the coat check ticket from the girl and slipped it into her clutch. Scanning the room, she noticed the large, centralized bar and decided that should be her first stop. A drink would give her something to do with her hand, and if it loosened her up, all the better.

Nervously adjusting her Mardi Gras–style mask, Lauren took a deep breath and headed to the bar. She ordered a dirty martini with extra olives and scoped out a dark corner where she could stand and do a little people-watching until she felt more comfortable.

She'd never been to one of these charity galas at the club before. These kinds of parties were for rich ranching families to mingle and make nice tax deductions. A food truck chef normally didn't have the time, energy or cash for something like this. As it was, she was already wincing at the cost of her drink. She supposed an open bar would cut too much into the charity's bottom line.

Most of the people there didn't seem to care. She'd overheard the man next to her at the bar tell the server to put it on his membership tab. A lot of others seemed to be doing that, too. The room was nearly filled to capacity with men in tuxedos and black Stetsons, women in sparkling gowns with ornately decorated masks. All of them had a cocktail in hand and a smile on their faces. At least, smiles on what you could see of their faces.

Masks were required for the event. At least, that was what the invitation said. Some wore smaller ones, Lone Ranger–style, which met the requirement, but you could still know who you were speaking to. She recognized a few people from around town even with them on. Others, like the man at the door, were wearing full-face masks. Lauren had opted for something in the middle, a black metal mask with ornate swirls cut out of it, that ended halfway down her face. It offered a little anonymity, but she didn't have to remove it to drink or eat.

And, as her meddling friend Amy had suggested, she wouldn't have to remove it to kiss, either.

Amy—ever the optimist when it came to Lauren's nonexistent love life. As though a new dress and a mask were enough for Lauren to fall into the strong arms of a dark, anonymous stranger.

Speaking of which, movement out of the corner of her gaze caught Lauren's attention. When she turned to look, she spied a tall drink of water heading toward her empty corner. He was wearing a beautifully tailored black tuxedo with a distinctive pewter wolf mask that brought out the platinum highlights in his cropped blond hair. All she could make out of his face was the hard square of his stubble-covered jaw and the flat line of displeasure that would otherwise be his mouth. The wolf wasn't having a good time tonight.

He wasn't looking at her. He had a cell phone pressed to one ear and his hand covering the other. If he was seeking privacy and quiet, he was out of luck. He glanced up at her for a moment, immediately dismissing her as he focused on his call and settled in the chair nearby.

Lauren wasn't about to give up her space to the big, bad wolf. She'd found it first. Perhaps she would venture out into the crowd in a moment, but she was only three sips into her twelve-dollar martini and she wasn't feeling bold enough quite yet.

But soon. She could feel the warmth of the alcohol spreading through her veins like the social lubricant that it was. Soon.

Sutton Wingate tried to check his troubles at the door tonight and have a good time, but they had still managed to follow him inside. Considering how things had gone the last few weeks, he wasn't sure why he was surprised.

When the accusations against his family had cropped up, he had been the optimistic one. As the CFO of Wingate Enterprises, he would know if there was embezzling and drug smuggling happening behind the scenes. There wasn't. It was just rumors fueled by jealousy and spite, and he was confident that eventually it would all blow over. He'd believed it right until the moment the Feds froze their assets, seized the ranch and put the whole family out on their asses.

Now he wasn't feeling so optimistic.

So far, everyone had landed on their feet. He and his twin, Sebastian, had decided to rent a house together. Luke and Ezekiel found places to stay. And his mother, Ava, was staying with Keith Cooper, a fact that no doubt pleased "Uncle" Keith. It wasn't an ideal situation, but they would persevere until they found out who was responsible for setting them up and their lives were returned to normal.

He thought losing the money and the family home would be the hardest thing to go through. At least until he walked through the door tonight.

His wolf mask did enough to hide his identity. If anyone suspected he might be a Wingate, they probably weren't sure if he was Sutton or Sebastian. But judging by the way people were gossiping about his family's scandal with him so nearby, no one knew who he was. He supposed that they didn't think the Wingates were bold enough to show up after everything that had happened. However, if they thought that, they clearly didn't know the Wingate family.

They were innocent and they would continue to act that way despite what others thought. Close friends seemed to be on Sutton's side, but he was stunned by how many "friends" had turned on them. He'd lost his job, his board position, his home… He'd even had to sell his collection of sports cars to have money to live on while the legal debacle carried on. He needed those friends now, more than ever. And they were drying up like a desert creek bed.

Sutton had been hoping for some good news

when his phone rang not long after arriving at the party. It was his attorney. Unfortunately, all his lawyer had to say was that he'd been unable to find a buyer for one of his cars and they might have to go to auction. He would lose money doing that, so he had to decide if he would live on what he had or if he had to cut his losses to make it through the financial tight spot they were in.

He wouldn't consider himself poor—he didn't expect anyone to cry for him because he only had one luxury sports car—but they certainly had stripped away a lot of the extravagances they were used to. He had plenty of investments tucked away, they all did, but cash was another matter. The team of lawyers they had working for them was funneling away everyone's money as quickly as they could come up with it.

Proving their innocence didn't come cheap.

"Just hold out a few more days. Maybe we'll get a buyer. I've got to go," Sutton said. Getting his long-winded attorney off the phone wasn't always so easy. When he finally succeeded, he slipped his phone into his breast pocket and sighed in dismay.

He could go rejoin the festivities and run the risk of hearing more ugly talk about his family. But at the moment, he had to say he was far more interested in the curvy brunette standing nearby. The red, beaded gown she'd chosen for the party clung to every hill and valley of her body and, at the moment, he was very grateful for the distraction.

If there was one thing Sutton appreciated more than the purring engine of an Italian sports car, it was women. Tall, short, thin, curvy…he had a fondness for them all. And with all the recent family drama, he hadn't had the time or energy to properly enjoy the opposite sex. The sultry brunette beside him was enough to remind him he was a man, not a machine, and he couldn't go on punishing himself forever.

At least tonight, he didn't have to be Sutton Wingate—scandal-plagued playboy and suspected drug trafficker. He wouldn't have to see the light of interest fade from a woman's eyes as she realized that the handsome man she was chatting with might very well have a one-way ticket to federal prison on the horizon. He was just a hungry wolf on the prowl for a tasty treat, just like Little Red Riding Hood here.

With a boost of confidence he hadn't felt in weeks, Sutton got up from his seat. He moved toward the woman, noticing that her glass was almost empty. "Are you on your way to your granny's house, Red?" he asked from just over her shoulder.

The woman turned to look at him and he was instantly struck by the curious, dark brown gaze that raked over him. The golden centers of her irises highlighted the movement even as the rest of her face was hidden from him. He waited on pins and needles for her response, hoping he would pass her inspection.

Her full, ruby lips smirked at him at last. "What big eyes you have," she said, playing along with his pick-up line.

"The better to see how thirsty you look, my dear."

"Do I look thirsty?" She gazed down at her glass. "I suppose I am."

"May I buy you a drink?"

"You may. A vodka martini, please." The woman plucked the skewer from her glass and he watched with anticipation as she sucked the last olive into her mouth. Her gaze didn't leave his as she chewed thoroughly and swallowed. She had one of the most sensuous mouths he'd ever seen. Maybe it was because it was all he could see, but he couldn't shake the image of pressing his lips against hers.

"Extra dirty," she added.

Sutton felt his heart stutter in his chest. Extra dirty, indeed. He had no idea who this goddess in red was, but she already had his undivided attention. Frankly, she could have anything she wanted, but they'd start with a delicious cocktail. "You've got it."

With a smile, he turned and strode over to the bar. He forced himself not to glance back over his shoulder as he did. He had a gnawing worry that if he peeked, she would be gone. A woman like that couldn't be real. Those curves, those lips, that sass… Maybe the mask added a layer of mystery to his lady in red, but there was more to it than that. There was an electricity, a chemistry between them that hit him like a ton of bricks the moment those big, brown eyes landed on him. He was completely under her spell.

At the bar, he caught the bartender's eye and ordered her dirty martini. "Put it on my tab," he said.

"I'd be happy to. But who are you?" the bartender asked, gesturing toward his eyes. "The masks," he explained.

"Oh, right. Wingate. Sutton."

"Gotcha. For a second, I thought you were Sebastian. I think you two have the same masks on tonight."

Sutton chuckled. "Yeah, we ordered both of them on Amazon at the last minute. Most folks can't tell us apart without a mask, so why make it easy on people tonight? Anyway, don't let him put any drinks on my tab."

The bartender chuckled and slid the dirty martini over to him. He was about to reach out and take the drink when he heard a muffled voice sounding over the crowd.

"Everyone, if you could please quiet down for just a moment, I have a few announcements before the evening goes on too much further."

Sutton turned to look at the stage where a woman in a black, lace gown was at the microphone stand. It was probably his sister Beth, who had organized the ball tonight.

She lifted up her black feathered mask and confirmed his suspicions. "Guess who?" she said with a chuckle that was echoed by the crowd.

"First, on behalf of Wingate Charities and those who benefit from our efforts, I'd like to thank all of you for purchasing a ticket and attending tonight. Despite everything, we are still dedicated to doing our good works for as long as we are able to. This branch of the company has been my baby, and it's very important to me, so I'd like to personally say thank you again for coming out to support us. I wasn't sure how many tickets or donations we would receive this year, but I never should've doubted the generous and thoughtful residents of Royal. In fact, this year we sold more tickets to the ball than ever before!"

Sutton knew the increased attendance this year probably had more to do with people hoping for a little juicy drama with their good cause, but he wouldn't say that to Beth and ruin her night. She worked hard to make the charity successful and she deserved the community's support, for whatever reason.

His sister paused for a bit of applause and to let her glistening eyes dry for a moment. "If you haven't already noticed, we have an amazing selection of donated items along the back wall as part of our silent auction. I encourage all of you to bid high and bid often," she said with a smile. "And, of course, we're also accepting good, old-fashioned checks. If you'd like to donate directly, you can find me near the coat check, where I have my handy receipt book ready. Gotta keep those accountants happy, right?

"Now, before we get back to the dancing, I have one more thing. My beautiful sister, Harley, and her fiancé, Grant Everett, have an announcement they'd like to share."

The couple came up to the stage with Beth and the band. Harley took the microphone that was extended to her and held it to her lips as she snuggled close to Grant's side. "Hello, everyone. I don't want to take too much time away from the celebration, but Grant and I wanted to share some exciting news. So many of you here are like family to us, and I feel like, lately, our family could use some happiness, so we will be getting married next month at the Everett family ranch. We won't have much time to print formal invitations, but we'll send out the details to everyone as soon as we can. We hope all of you will come celebrate with us."

The crowd cheered appropriately. Sutton figured half the applause was genuine, half was polite. Like this party, some people in this town would attend just to see if anything gossip-worthy happened at the wedding. He doubted it. Harley was used to getting her way and she wouldn't allow anything, even the family's hard times, to ruin her wedding. She'd already had to concede on the location. Harley had wanted to marry at the Wingate Estate, but they had no idea how long it would be—if ever—before they could step foot back on the property. Apparently she and Grant had decided not to wait and find out. The wedding was already five years late as it was.

His family departed from the stage as the music started up again. That was Sutton's cue to take his drink and turn back to this evening's beautiful distraction. He let a heavy sigh of relief escape his lungs when he turned and found his mystery woman was still there waiting for him.

"Extra dirty," he said, handing her the glass.

"You or the drink?" she asked with a twinkle in her dark eyes.

Sutton clucked his tongue in appreciation. Her flirting game was top-notch and he wasn't easily impressed. He was certain he knew everyone in this town and all the members of the club for sure, but this woman was new and exciting in every way. Perhaps she wasn't from around here. That would be even better. If she was a visitor to Royal, she wouldn't know about the Wingates and their hard times.

"Maybe both," he drawled. "I am the big, bad wolf after all."

"Good." She smiled and took a sip of her new drink.

Two

Cinderella Sweepstakes, indeed. Lauren was pretty certain that she'd been sucked into some kind of fairy tale. But instead of a royal ball, it was a charity gala in Royal and, instead of a prince, she was dancing with the big, bad wolf in an Armani tuxedo. She kept waiting to lose a shoe and turn into a pumpkin, but midnight came and went, and the smooth, seductive prince was still holding her in his arms.

She couldn't believe it. Or how she was behaving. There was a certain magic to the mask she hadn't expected when she'd put it on that night. It made her feel bold. Brazen. And beyond reckless.

Combined with the dark press of the dance floor, the mask made words flow freely from her lips that she'd never dream of saying without it.

Her masked suitor hadn't left her side all night. They'd danced, perused the silent auction offerings and nibbled on plates of hors d'oeuvres they'd selected between dances. It was a nice spread rife with cocktail shrimp, sweet-and-spicy meatballs, crostini with caviar, and endive with lump crab and blue cheese. It lacked a certain something that as a chef she noticed, but she wouldn't dare say as much.

Instead, she ate what she could, hoping some food would help keep her stomach from flip-flopping in her gown. It wasn't helping, though, because it wasn't an empty tummy or too much alcohol that was causing her squirrely stomach. It was nerves.

The night was winding down. Judging by the way her companion held her when they danced, their time together was building up to something. Was she ready for it? When those green eyes looked at her through that mask, she felt a pull deep inside.

Yes.

She was ready for anything her handsome masked suitor had to offer. Tonight she was going to do what she felt like doing. Not what was best for the business. What was best for *Lauren*. And she couldn't come up with a single reason why giving herself body and soul to the sexy, articulate man holding her in his arms was a bad idea. She'd given so many years to her business, denying her body the closeness it craved to another person. She was tired of being lonely.

The song they were dancing to ended and instead of pulling away, her dancing partner drew her closer. The feel of his hard, muscular body pressing into her made her pulse start to race. She was probably blushing like mad beneath her mask, not that he could see it. She wrapped her arms around his neck and pressed her breasts against the firm wall of his chest.

His jaw flexed as he looked down at her and took a ragged breath. "Come with me, Red," he said.

There was something different in the way he looked at her now. He wasn't asking her to come with him to get a drink or bid on a gift basket. No, she knew what he was asking and she was eager to comply. She took the hand he held out to her and let him lead her off the dance floor.

They cut through the crowds and deeper into the club instead of moving to the door.

"Where are we going?" she whispered. She wasn't very familiar with the club, but it was clear to her that he was as they went down a dark hallway. She felt her nerves increase as they disappeared into the back of the building. She had to tell herself he was looking for privacy, not a good laugh, to keep her feet moving in step behind his.

"I thought you might be interested in shooting

a little pool." He opened a door and they stepped into the dark room.

She felt her body start to relax when she glimpsed the moonlight coming through a window, highlighting the large, oak billiard table in the center of the room. Around the edge were bar-height tables and racks filled with pool cues on the wall. It seemed just likc the kind of space where filthy-rich cowboys would sit around, drink a beer or some whiskey and shoot a few games together.

Lauren walked into the room and let her manicured fingers drag along the felt top of the heavy, wooden pool table. She set her purse aside, turned back to face him and leaned against the edge. "Really?" she said with a sly smile that betrayed the butterflies swarming inside of her. "You brought me back here to this dark, private room so we could play...*pool*?"

The light from the hallway highlighted his amused smile until he shut the door and the heavy blackness of the night hid it away. "Not exactly."

She could just make out the shape of him as he slipped out of his tuxedo jacket and tossed it over the nearby bar stool. "But I thought perhaps we could play a little game."

"I'm listening," she purred, hoping her coy words would cover how nervous she was.

"I was thinking something a little more intimate than billiards. Something where we both can win."

"Will there still be wood, balls and the occasional scratching involved in your game?"

"God, I hope so," he said under his breath. "What do you say?"

"It sounds like fun. I'm in. But I have one condition."

He straightened up and put his hands in his pockets. "And what's that, Red?"

"The masks stay on and the lights stay off." She wanted to keep up the mystery for both of them. Her bravado would crumble without it to hide behind. She might be willing to give this man her body, but being in this place again after all these years, she needed to keep a piece of herself protected.

He didn't answer. Instead, he moved closer to her, hesitating for only a moment before picking her up and lifting her fully onto the pool table. She let out a startled whoop as she landed, reaching for him to steady herself. He was all too eager to pull her close.

"Wow," she whispered against his throat.

She heard him chuckle softly before he pulled away just a bit. "I hope that's not the last time you say that tonight."

Then his lips found hers for the first time and her head started swimming so wildly from the intensity of their kiss that the next few minutes were a dark, pleasurable blur. His mouth never left hers as her beaded gown was pushed up her legs.

"How do you like the game so far?" he rasped, nestling himself between her thighs and cupping her ass with his hands to tug her hips hard against the throbbing erection pressing against his trousers.

Lauren gasped at the feeling of him pressed so intimately against her and then wrapped her legs around his waist to keep him there. "It's way better than billiards."

She leaned in to kiss him again and, as she nipped gently at his bottom lip, they quickly reached the point of no return. This was really, *truly* happening. Sex with a stranger. In public. The thought was enough to send a shiver through her whole body in anticipation. Their hands explored each other's unfamiliar bodies, fighting with buttons and zippers, tugging aside cotton and satin until each finally made contact with the naked skin they desperately sought out.

Lauren couldn't get enough of her masked man. With his tuxedo shirt open to the waist, she found he was hard in all the right places with rough patches of hair on his chest that tickled her palms. The warm scent of his skin teased at her senses, urging her to bury her face in his throat and taste him. The growl that rumbled from deep inside his chest vibrated against her lips and fingertips. She might not be an expert where seduction was concerned, but it sounded like she was hitting all the right buttons with him.

The wolf's hands moved over her outer thighs, pushing the heavy fabric of her gown higher. "Lift your hips, Red," he said, and she complied. Now the dress was bunched around her waist, giving him free access to everything from there down.

That was exactly how he must've wanted it. His fingers grasped the sides of her panties and tugged them down her legs, stopping long enough to slip off her rhinestone-covered heels and let them fall to the floor along with the panties in his hand.

Had the lights been on, Lauren would've felt incredibly exposed, but in the dark there was a freedom she didn't expect. Her partner could only see with his hands, something that would greatly benefit her, of that she was certain.

As he stood up, his hands smoothed back over her legs. He dipped to the inside of her knees and stroked the skin of her inner thighs even as he inched them farther apart. Lauren could feel the cool air on her newly exposed flesh, but to her surprise it was quickly followed by the moist heat of his breath.

She wasn't prepared for his tongue.

Lauren gasped and squirmed against the hard edge of the pool table. With each flick of his tongue across her aching flesh, her mind went blank to everything but the waves of pleasure that pulsated through her body. She had to lean back onto her elbows before she collapsed entirely. Her back arched, her hands clawing futilely at the felt top. In mere moments, this stranger had coaxed heady sensations from her that she could hardly remember having before. He had her on the edge of climax and he'd barely touched her.

"Lie back and relax," he commanded, briefly lifting his head. Lauren couldn't do anything but comply. The man moved each of her legs over his shoulders, pushing her knees backward until they were pressed to her chest. With her pinned there, he unleashed a fresh assault on her center.

It was unlike anything she'd ever felt before. She couldn't escape the sensations, couldn't pull away from his mouth. Before she knew it, an orgasm washed over her that was stronger than any one she'd ever had. She bit into the side of her hand to keep from screaming out loud until the waves passed. But he didn't stop. He let up for only a moment, allowing her to catch her breath before he started again. She didn't think it was possible, but she came again almost immediately, harder than before.

"Please stop," she gasped and pressed against his head to push him away. Lauren wasn't sure she could take a third orgasm so soon.

He relented, lowering her legs and allowing them to fall like limp noodles over the edge of the table. "You've had enough?" he asked.

"Enough of that. Now I want you. Or are you going to keep me waiting?"

He stood up, resting his hands on her shaky knees. "Not too much longer. I've just got to take care of one, important, final detail."

Lauren watched as the dark shape of his body moved across the room to where he'd left his tuxedo jacket. He dug around in the pockets for a moment before returning to her still-trembling body.

Stepping back between her thighs, he put something on the pool table beside her bare hip. The moonlight caught the foil packaging to reveal the condom he'd sought out. Thankfully, he planned for things like this. It was so unlike Lauren to do something like this that she never would've had condoms in her purse.

She heard the clinking of his belt and the buzz of him undoing his zipper. Felt him reach for the condom to put it on. Then his hands gripped her hips and he entered her in one, slow, steady stroke. The hard heat of him sinking into her welcoming body was a pleasure she'd long denied herself. Building her business hadn't allowed her much of a social life. She dated now and then, but nothing serious. How could she date in a town where all her peers thought she was a joke? It wasn't impossible, but it had been so long, she almost couldn't believe it was really happening.

Lauren pushed herself upright on the edge of the

table, wrapping her legs around his waist and her arms around his neck. Pressing her satin-covered breasts against the wall of his chest, she leaned in and whispered, "I need you so badly," before gently biting at his earlobe.

He must've liked it because he shuddered in her arms and stilled himself, perhaps to regain control. She was pretty sure he was fighting a losing battle, because this fantasy had them both riding the razor edge of desire. He gripped her back and pulled Lauren so close to the precipice that she might have fallen without his support. Then he gave her what she'd asked for. He filled her again and again, pounding hard into her quaking body.

He didn't know her name or anything about her, but he seemed to know exactly what Lauren needed from him. She didn't think it was possible to respond to him so quickly, but she was on the edge of coming apart again. She clung to her big, bad wolf, gasping and whimpering into his shoulder.

As Lauren's release came closer, her body tensed and her cries sharpened. He responded by redoubling his efforts and thrusting harder than ever before. She instantly unraveled, shattering into climax as she bit into the flesh of his shoulder to silence her screams. When she was finally silent and still, he thrust hard one last time and finished with a deep groan of satisfaction.

They collapsed back onto the pool table together,

and after a moment he rolled off to the side to rest beside her and catch his breath. It was strange to lie there together in the pitch-darkness of the room, hearing the voices and music from the great room just feet down the hall from where they were.

She expected the wolf to say something, but they both seemed comfortable enough in the silence. Perhaps too comfortable. After a few minutes, his breathing was steady and even. He'd fallen asleep beside her. She was tempted to curl against him and give in to the lure of sleep, too. But she needed to go.

The morning would bring nothing but disappointment for them both. Lauren knew it deep down. She was not the glamorous seductress she'd pretended to be tonight. She'd never acted more out of character in her whole life. Staying behind meant that her lover would learn the truth. And that would ruin everything.

Moving as quietly as she could, Lauren slipped off the table. She shimmied her dress down her legs and then sought out her things in the darkness.

Looking back over her shoulder, she could see he was still fast asleep on the table. She pulled her mask off and tossed it onto the felt beside him. A little memento for him to remember her by.

With that done, she opened the door and crept out into the hallway and out of his life.

* * *

“What the—”

Sutton groaned and pushed up onto his elbows. Every muscle in his body ached in a way he’d never felt before and he’d been awakened by a pain in his lower back that was strong enough to rouse him. It felt like he’d been sleeping on a wooden plank or something. Looking around the dark room, it all came back to him. He was still in the club billiard room and he had, in fact, been sleeping on a wooden plank. He’d fallen asleep on the pool table after making love to his dance partner. He lifted his wrist and squinted in the dark at the face of his Rolex. It was four thirty in the morning.

He turned his head toward the spot where she’d lain beside him. The room was still dark, but he couldn’t make out the shape of her there. He stretched his arm out across the soft, felt surface of the table, but it just kept going. The surface was cold, with no trace of her warm, supple body beside him. Then his fingertips brushed against something.

Sitting up, Sutton slid off the table and crossed the room to switch on the light. He winced for a moment before his eyes adjusted and he could see what was left behind on the table. It was her mask. He walked over to pick it up and, once he did, he held it in his hands for a moment.

He knew then that Red was long gone. And he

had no way of ever knowing who she was or how to find her again.

Dammit.

With her gone, the novelty of the darkness and anonymity of their encounter wasn't as exciting. Now it was just frustrating as hell. That woman—that red-gowned goddess—was the greatest thing to happen to him in a long time. They had a connection unlike anything he'd felt with another woman before. And now he had nothing to show for their encounter but a stiff back and an ornate, black mask.

He sighed and tossed the mask onto the pool table. Then he focused on gathering up the rest of his clothes and putting them back on. His own mask was on the floor with his tie. He picked it up and threw it into the trash can. He wasn't going to hide anymore. Not from the small-minded people in town who wanted to believe the worst of him and not from anyone else. His desire to escape from reality, even for just one night, had cost him his chance to have something...special. Maybe the kind of relationship he'd never had before.

As crazy as it sounded, somehow he knew it was true. His playboy reputation in Royal was well earned, but last night was different. *She* was different. He didn't wake up satiated and ready to tackle the next challenge. Rather, he felt like he'd been robbed in his sleep. He'd already lost his home and fortune, but somehow this hurt even worse. He wasn't used to this feeling. To losing. But it was all he seemed to do lately.

Sutton picked up her mask and looked at it again. A part of him wanted to throw it out along with his own. It was probably better that he forget all about tonight and about her. He and his family had enough to deal with right now without him adding unnecessary drama. But he couldn't bring himself to toss it away. It was all he had left of her. Instead, he stuffed it into his pocket and headed to the door. He needed to take a cue from Cinderella and get out of here before he had to do the walk of shame through a lobby full of folks who were there to play an early-morning round of golf.

As he stepped out into the hallway, he found the rest of the club was as dark and quiet as the room he'd come from. The party had ended a long time ago. Some dim lighting around the bar area highlighted the broken-down tables and equipment that were stacked up to be carried off in the morning. It also highlighted a familiar, slumped figure sitting at the bar.

"Sebastian? Is that you?"

The figure turned toward him and lifted his mask up so that it sat on top of his head. Yes, it was his twin brother, Sebastian, looking exhausted and depressed as he clutched a glass of something in his hand. "Sutton?" He frowned in confusion. "What are you doing here so late?"

"I just woke up. I passed out in the billiard room. Why are you still here?"

His twin shook his head and sighed sadly. "I was with a woman tonight. An amazing woman. A dream in red that I would marry on the spot if she'd have me. But she disappeared before I could even get her name."

Sutton frowned at the all-too-familiar story. What were the odds that both of them would have an incredible night with a woman in red that fled at the first chance? It was an uncanny coincidence, but perhaps it was just that kind of a night. Maybe there was something in the air. "Okay, but why are you sitting at the bar at this hour instead of going home?"

Sebastian shrugged. "Well, when I woke up alone, I came back to the bar to pour myself a drink and commiserate over my bad luck with women. So I've just been sitting here thinking about everything that happened tonight. About her and how captivating she was. I've never met another woman like her, Sutton." He shook his head sadly. "And then I started thinking about everything going on with the company and the feds. Time got away from me, I guess."

"We've both got a lot on our minds."

His brother nodded and then turned to look at him curiously. "How did you fall asleep in the billiard room?" he asked, as though he'd finally processed his brother's words from minutes before.

"I was back there with a woman. She ran off, too. Seems we both had amazing nights with women who would rather we not call them the next day."

"Do you *ever* call them the next day?"

Sutton frowned at his brother. When it came to romance, he and his twin couldn't be more different. "I resent that implication. There are many women around town that may have loved and lost me over the years, dear brother, but I was always a gentleman in the end. I've never left a woman scorned."

Sebastian looked at him as though he didn't quite believe Sutton's version of events, but shook his head before saying so. "Well, it sounds like you got a little bit of your own medicine tonight. She left you wanting more for once, huh?"

That was an understatement. But it was too late to be philosophizing about dating karma and how it had made its way back to Sutton with a vengeance.

"Are you hungry?" he asked, changing the subject.

Sebastian shrugged. "I guess I could eat. All those appetizers didn't really add up to dinner."

He slapped his brother on the back and fished his keys out of his suit-coat pocket. "Come on, then. I'll drive us to the Royal Diner and treat you to an early breakfast before we head home. Maybe we can beat the sunrise."

Three

"Looks like someone had a good time last night."

Lauren winced at the daylight that flooded into the food truck as Amy opened the door and climbed inside. She regarded her employee for a moment and then returned to her steaming-hot cup of coffee. "I guess."

"You were out late," Amy noted. "Drinking and schmoozing with Royal's elite, no doubt."

"Yes. I got home very late and I had several martinis. So you'll have to excuse me if I'm not leaping for joy this morning. I'm exhausted, I have a headache and my feet still hurt from the ridiculous heels that woman picked out for me. I should've just worn my Converse under the dress. No one would've seen them but me."

"Well, even hungover you still look amazing," her friend told her. "That makeover they gave you was something else. If it wasn't for that early-morning sneer I recognize, I couldn't be certain it was really you."

It was too early and Lauren was too tired to be flattered by Amy's backward compliment. "Very funny. I suppose I do clean up alright, but looking hot doesn't do me any good when it comes to being a chef."

"I don't know about that. I'd say you're hot enough to get a Food Network show, now."

Lauren perked up in her seat at the ridiculous statement. "A TV show? I can't even get the capital raised for a restaurant. No network executive is going to be interested in giving me a television platform."

"Not with that frown. But you should've hit up some of those people at the party last night to see if they wanted to invest." Amy slapped down the Sunday paper onto the stainless steel counter with a chuckle. "It seems like it was quite the shindig. They raised a fortune for the Wingate Charity. Those rich folks know how to party. And write checks. You should've held your hand out."

Lauren reached for the paper and scanned the article on the front page about the masquerade ball.

Most of it was about the charity and the good works they were planning with the funds raised at the event. The photo above the fold was of the event coordinator, Beth Wingate, and a man in a familiar wolf mask identified by the article's author as her brother and the CEO of Wingate Enterprises, Sebastian Wingate.

The information hit her gut with a dull thud that threatened to send her coffee back up. She'd thought she might never know the identity of the man she'd been with last night. And had figured that perhaps it was better that way. After all, last night was a moment in time between two people that could never be replicated. Trying to would only ruin the memory of what they'd shared.

And yet, now that she'd looked down at the name in black-and-white print, she couldn't ignore what she'd seen. The genie wouldn't go back into the bottle once it was out. Her mysterious lover was none other than the man at the center of all the town drama lately. Lauren didn't know much about the Wingates and couldn't pick them out of a lineup if her life depended on it, but she'd heard the name more than a few times recently. The family had been accused of drug smuggling and other ugly things and the whole town was buzzing about it.

No wonder her mystery man had looked so irritated on the phone when she'd first laid eyes on him.

That was just Lauren's luck. She has a whirlwind

romance with a rich, successful guy and it turns out that he's really broke and on his way to federal prison. She should've taken the hint when her suitor was wearing a wolf's mask. No good could come from that. Every fairy tale proved that much.

"So tell me everything," Amy pressed.

"I'd rather hear about how things went with the trucks last night." Lauren had left her two precious Street Eats food trucks in her trusted employee's hands on the busiest night of the week. That was a far more important topic to discuss.

"Well, Javier's truck got robbed at gunpoint and my undercooked shrimp gave ten people food poisoning, but I think it went well enough, all things considered."

Lauren looked at her friend and the deadly serious expression on her face. She knew it meant nothing—Amy was notorious for messing with her. "Seriously. Come on, now."

"Everything went fine." Amy relented with a heavy sigh. "The biggest drama of the night was running out of chicken kebabs pretty early. Other than that, things went smoothly and Javier made the nightly deposit, no problems. Now, tell me about this fancy shindig. I'm dying to know how it went for you."

"We're not here to gossip. We're here to head over to the farmers market to get fresh produce for this afternoon's menu."

The other woman just shrugged. “There’s no rule that says you can’t spill your guts while we peruse the day’s vegetables. Come on, I entered you in that contest. No fair to go and not share every delicious detail with me.”

“You should’ve come as my plus-one if you were so interested,” Lauren said as she picked up her coffee and shopping list. She stopped by the door to grab her foldable handcart so she could haul back vegetables.

“Someone had to run the trucks,” Amy sassed from over her shoulder. “And besides that, no one has ever gotten into the good kind of trouble with their friend clinging on.”

They climbed out of the food truck and Lauren slammed and locked the door behind them. “Whatever,” she muttered, turning in the direction of the farmers market and pointedly ignoring that Amy had been absolutely right in her assessment.

“*Whatever?* That’s all I get?” Amy kept her pace at Lauren’s side, her long, blond ponytail swinging in the breeze as they walked. “You know I’m not letting this go, right?”

“Have you ever?”

“No,” Amy quipped.

That was about right. Amy was a dog with a bone and she always seemed to think she knew what was right for Lauren. She stayed out of the business affairs and let Lauren take full rein over the menu, but when it came to her personal life, her best friend had a lot to say about it.

Thankfully, the farmers market was busy and loud. “When we’re done,” she promised. “I’m not talking about it here. Pick out a nice crate of sweet potatoes and a couple bushels of tomatoes and onions. I’m going to get broccoli, cauliflower and check out thc apples.”

They met up about fifteen minutes later near the booth of one of the local ranchers. They usually had a nice selection of locally raised, harvested and smoked meats, and today was no exception. Lauren got a dozen eggs, a large pork shoulder, chicken breasts and some nice, thick-cut bacon.

“What’s on the menu for today?” Amy asked as they hauled their wares back to the trucks.

“I don’t know yet,” Lauren admitted. She had to see what looked good and what was seasonally at peak. Then she would find a way to combine it all into a few dishes for the next day or so. “I was thinking of some chipotle sweet potato fries for a start. Maybe pair it with barbecue chicken kebabs since they did so well yesterday. I might change up the spices a little. Carnitas tacos with a bacon crema and fresh tomato salsa. Perhaps some spicy deep-fried broccoli and cauliflower to go with it. Apple hand pies for dessert. I’ll have to look at what we have and think on it some more.”

“Sounds good to me.”

Once everything was hauled into the truck, they started cleaning and prepping for the day. Lauren was relieved to fall into the familiar drudgery of her work routine and not have to think about last night for a little while longer. They were up to their elbows in a crate of sweet potatoes when they heard a knock at the window.

Lauren approached the serving door, preparing to tell whomever it was that they wouldn't be serving until 11:30 a.m., but found Gracie Diaz there with a smile on her face and her favorite pumpkin spice latte in her hand. The newest Royal millionaire was one of Street Eats's biggest fans. She used to show up at the trucks at least a few times a week, after work with the Wingates. Now that she didn't have to earn a living, Gracie had been a bit scarcer. Lauren missed her coming by and was glad to see her again.

"Hey, Gracie," she said, sliding open the window. "Haven't seen you in a little while. How's the millionaire life been treating you?"

"It's—" Gracie hesitated for a moment with a conflicted expression on her face "—not what I expected. But I won't complain about something like that. No one has any sympathy for my problems anyway."

Lauren nodded. The path to Gracie's lottery win had been complicated, but now she could hopefully enjoy the fruits of her success. "More money, more problems, right? Well, if you get tired of rich people and feel like hanging out with us lowly food truck cooks, you know how to find us."

Gracie held up her phone. "I always know where you guys are parked for the day, even if I can't make it over. And you're not a cook, Lauren. You're a chef. An *amazing* chef. The food trucks are a means to an cnd and one day you're going to have a restaurant without wheels. I know it."

"From your lips," Lauren said with a smile.

"I'm surprised you're going to be open today, though. You went to the masquerade ball last night, didn't you? I'd heard you won that contest, so I half expected you to close the trucks down for today and rest. That was a late night for everyone."

She had no idea. Lauren had gotten a whopping four hours of sleep after slinking home and lying in bed for longer than necessary, thinking about what she'd just done. It had been the single most erotic encounter of her entire life. Every time she closed her eyes, she could feel his hands on her body again. It took hours for the adrenaline to wear off and allow her to sleep at last.

"It was more exciting than I expected it to be when I won the contest. I had a good time," she said, avoiding any unnecessary details. "How about you?"

Gracie smiled with a wistful look in her eye. She looked down at her latte and took a sip, avoiding Lauren's gaze. "It was fun. It almost felt like the kind of night that could change your life forever if you'd let it."

She was startled by her on-point observation. What did she mean by that? Gracie couldn't even look her in the eye as she said the words. Had she seen Lauren with Sebastian last night? It's possible that Lauren was the only outsider who hadn't recognized the infamous CEO on sight, even with his mask. Perhaps the whole town's tongues were wagging about her torrid hookup in the billiard room and Gracie was giving her a heads-up before it all hit the proverbial fan.

If that was the case, she might need to reach out to Sebastian and do some damage control. Seeing him again would be a scary and exciting prospect. His woman in red was long gone, but she would have to do it. She'd worked very hard to build her business and she didn't want one night's indiscretions to ruin it all. She'd gone to that party to make connections, not to become gossip fodder.

She pushed her worries aside for the moment. Right now she needed to focus on getting the menu going and getting the staff prepped for the trucks going out today. But sooner or later, Lauren would have to face the music and track down Sebastian Wingate.

It was a Monday morning. Typically one of the busiest mornings of the week. And yet Sebastian

Wingate had nothing to do. He'd gotten up early, as he always did. Ran a few miles. Then showered, had some coffee and ate his breakfast. Now he had run out of things to do with his time.

Sutton had already left the house. He'd gone into town to talk to his lawyer about one of the cars he was trying to sell. His twin seemed much more comfortable with his free time. At least, he was better at finding ways to fill the hours. Sebastian was counting down each minute that went by until their reputation and board positions were restored. Then life could get back to normal.

It would happen. He kept telling himself as much. But until then, he needed something to do with his time. Maybe he could make a few calls and round up some guys to play eighteen holes over at Pine Valley. He picked up his phone and realized quickly that everyone he knew was at work.

Frustrated, he finished off his second cup of coffee and put the mug into the sink. He had to get out of this rental house before he went stir-crazy. Grabbing the keys to his BMW from the counter and his jacket from the hall closet, he went to the front door and flung it open—completely scaring the hell out of the woman standing there, about to ring the doorbell.

Sebastian had nearly collided with her in his haste. "I'm so sorry," he said, taking a step back into the house while they both recovered from the unexpected near miss.

He took the moment to study the unanticipated visitor. Once the flush of excitement faded, he noticed that the woman standing on his stoop was quite pretty. The sun made the honey highlights in her brown hair shine. She had full lips and a full figure beneath the leather jacket and clingy jeans she was wearing. But he didn't recognize her.

"It's my fault," she insisted. "I've been standing here working up the nerve to ring the doorbell."

"I'm not sure who you're looking for, but we just rented this house," he explained. She looked at him like she knew him somehow, but he couldn't place her.

"Actually, I think you're the one I'm looking for. Are you Sebastian Wingate?"

Suspicion suddenly crept into his mind. He hated that he had started looking for dark intentions in everyone he met, but it couldn't be helped. Someone had set his family up and, until they found out who it was, everyone was a potential suspect. "If I said that I was Sebastian Wingate, would you serve me a subpoena?"

The woman's dark eyes grew wide with surprise. "No! A subpoena? Not at all."

Her reaction seemed genuine enough. "Okay, then. Yes, I'm Sebastian Wingate. What can I do for you?"

The woman seemed to grow a little more nervous as he looked at her. She chewed at her full bottom lip anxiously for a moment before taking a breath and seemingly steeling her nerves. "My name is Lauren Roberts. I own a couple food trucks here in town. Street Eats, if you've heard of it. I specialize in high-end, local ingredients, in a fresh, easy-to-eat style..."

Sebastian nodded as she continued to talk, although he wasn't certain why a lady who owned food trucks was coming to see him. She certainly wasn't hunting down investors, or if she was, she hadn't done her homework. The Wingates were not the honeypot they'd been only a few short weeks ago.

"...none of that is really important—" she stopped at last to take a breath "—I'm actually here because you and I, um, *met* at the party Saturday night."

Sebastian met a lot of people at the party Saturday night. But judging by the way the woman was looking at him expectantly, this had been no ordinary meeting.

"You and I—" she hesitated again "—slept together."

Now it was Sebastian's turn to be wide-eyed with surprise. Saturday night had been amazing. One of the most incredible nights of his life. But he hadn't anticipated the mysterious woman to just show up on his doorstep. That was a gift he had never expected to receive.

"Oh, wow," he said, anxiously running his fingers through his hair. "Please come in."

Lauren stepped into the house, waiting as he shut the door and escorted her inside to the living room. "I know you were on your way out, so I understand if you can't talk right now."

"No, no," he insisted. "I was just going to get out of the house for a little while. I have time." Nothing but time, actually. Especially for the vision in red that had been on his mind since she walked out on him that night. "Please have a seat."

She chose the armchair, so he opted to settle into the couch beside her. "Can I get you a drink or something?"

"No, I'm fine, thank you. I just came here to talk to you for a moment in private. I didn't realize who you were until I saw your photo in the newspaper the next day. When I saw your name there, I knew that I needed to come see you and explain—"

"Explain what?" he interrupted. As far as he could recall, what had happened between them was the textbook definition of one thing leading to another. They couldn't have stopped it from happening if they'd tried.

"To explain to you that everything I did that night was out of character for me. I don't want you to think that I'm the kind of woman that normally acts that way." She shook her head as the embarrassed pink returned to her cheeks.

"That's not the kind of thing I normally do either," he admitted. "I leave the escapades to my brother. But with everything going on, I was out of sorts and acted uncharacteristically. Under normal circumstances, I'm more of a gentleman. Considering that we didn't take off our masks and I didn't even get your name… Well, that's very unlike me."

Lauren sighed, seeming to relax a little bit. "I just wanted you to know that, in case people started talking about seeing us together and tongues started wagging."

"People are always talking about me, so I'm used to it," Sebastian replied. Though it was worse than normal lately. "But like I said, I'm not a one-night stand kind of guy. It sounds like you aren't either, so what about going out again?"

It hadn't been what he thought he would propose when they sat down in the living room, but faced with the prospect of this fetching woman walking out the door again, he realized he couldn't bear it. "What about dinner? We can get to know each other better. Maybe Saturday night can turn into more for us."

Lauren seemed a little stunned by his proposal, but she recovered quickly with a smile and a nod. "That would be nice. My trucks don't run Wednesdays, so that's one of the few evenings I have free."

"Okay. Wednesday night it is." He reached for his phone and they exchanged numbers. "I'll see if I can get us reservations at The Glass House around seven and then I'll text you to confirm the time. Send me your address and I'll be by to pick you up."

"You don't have to do that," Lauren insisted.

"Of course, I do. It's a date. We may have put the cart before the horse, but I intend to correct that and do things right this time around."

"Alright, if you insist." Lauren stood up suddenly, prompting Sebastian to do the same. "I guess I will see you Wednesday night, then." She thrust out her hand toward him to say goodbye.

It seemed a ridiculously awkward and distant gesture between two people who had been as intimate as it gets, but as they'd said, they were both different people that night. They were starting over without masks and alcohol to muddy the waters. While a friendly hug or a kiss on the cheek might be more appropriate, he wasn't going to push her for more and run her off a second time. He reached out and shook her hand softly, and then escorted her out the door.

As he shut it behind her, he looked down at his hand and frowned. Something wasn't quite right.

He couldn't put his finger on it, but something had changed between them since Saturday. At the club that night, he couldn't stop touching her. There was something magnetic between them that drew him closer every time he tried to pull away. Every graze across her bare skin sent sparks through his whole nervous system. He'd never felt something like that with a woman in his entire life.

That couldn't all be chalked up to alcohol and the novelty of masks. That was chemistry, plain and simple. And chemistry wasn't something that was there one day and gone the next. It pulled you back again and again, even when you knew you should stay away. That was the kind of passion and desire he'd felt for the dark-haired beauty he'd held in his arms that night.

And now it was all gone. Kaput.

He hated to admit it, but Lauren might as well have been a random stranger at the office or the store. Pretty, no doubt. Personable, albeit nervous. But when he'd shaken her hand, there had been no tingles, no chills. Her hands were soft and nicely manicured, but if he had closed his eyes and touched her, he wouldn't have said she was the woman from the party.

And yet she'd shown up on his doorstep insisting that she was the one. No one else knew about what happened that night but the two of them. So if Lauren said she was the woman he'd shared the evening with, it had to be true.

Sebastian hoped perhaps the chemistry would return once they became more familiar with each other and she could finally relax. Maybe a glass of wine would take the edge off and their attraction would flow freely again. He'd been given a second chance and he wanted more than anything for his masked beauty to be back in his arms.

But if the blazing attraction didn't return, Sebastian would be sorely disappointed.

Four

Lauren was just nervous. Yeah. That was it.

There was no other explanation for why this was quite possibly the most boring date she'd ever been on in her life. She was dining with a handsome, rich and powerful man at the best and most expensive restaurant in town. It shouldn't be that hard to have a good time. The food had been amazing and the wine deliciously paired with each course. Sebastian was an excellent conversationalist, getting even her introverted self to talk freely. And he was also charming and polite, favoring her with that same beautiful smile she remembered from their first night together. They'd had a nice enough time.

It just didn't feel like a *date.* It felt like dinner with a friend from out of town. Pleasant enough, but not charged with that same undeniable spark of attraction that had left her breathless from the moment they'd first met.

Now the green eyes she'd lost herself in at the gala were studying her across the table as they finished their desserts. The same chiseled jawline she'd kissed was moving gently as he chewed the last bite of his cheesecake. Every physical indication pointed toward Sebastian being the man she was with that night. Everything but the most important part—the chemistry.

After he paid the check, they walked around the beautifully designed grounds of the Bellamy Hotel for a while. The weather was cooler, but the skies were clear, making for a pleasant fall evening for Texas. She might have even enjoyed the stroll if not for the pressure she'd put on herself for tonight to be special. And, of course, for the heels from the party she'd worn again, as though some magical shoes would make the difference.

Once again, they didn't do much more than pinch her toes and make her regret wearing them. They were going in the donation pile the minute she got home.

They finally made their way back to Sebastian's car, and with no other reason to continue their night together, he drove her back to her small home, far from the luxurious ranches and expensive mansions of Pine Valley. Her place was small and much more modest in every respect except the kitchen. She had it remodeled to suit a chef and now it likely rivaled even the most expensive home in Royal. You wouldn't know it when you looked at the outside of the house, though.

He pulled into her driveway and, like the gentleman he was, ran around the car to open her door and then escorted her up the cobblestone walkway to her front porch. It was nice, but her big, bad wolf hadn't been entirely a gentleman. He'd taken what she'd freely given and she missed that intensity tonight. She missed everything from their first night together.

"Sebastian," she said as she stopped on her doorstep and turned around to face him. He was following close behind, but thankfully not too close. She didn't think he'd be asking for a kiss or anything more tonight.

"Yes?"

"I had a nice time this evening."

"I did, too," he said with a blankly polite smile that proved to her that he was as unimpressed with their date as she was.

She felt like an obligation to him, and that was worse than their lack of sexual attraction. She had to end this before they wasted any more time just being courteous. "And I appreciate you making an effort to turn our night together into more. But I'm not sure we should go out again."

His expression was mildly surprised. "Are you breaking up with me? I've never been dumped in my life."

"I wouldn't say *dumped*," she corrected. Lauren didn't want to be known as the only woman dumb enough to break it off with Sebastian Wingate. "I'd say we parted ways by mutual decision. You can't tell me that you had an amazing time tonight and can't wait to see me again."

"Well, no," he admitted sheepishly. "But I've had worse dates. And I don't know that I'm ready to give up on us so soon. It was just one night. Maybe we should do something different next time. Something a little less formal and stuffy. I think we both put too much pressure on ourselves to make this date successful." He cleared his throat. "How about we drive up to Dallas and do something fun? There's plenty of restaurants, museums and other things to do there."

Lauren studied his face and felt conflicted by his words. He was trying. He really was. But if it was only out of obligation, she didn't want any part in it. So, they had a night of hot, anonymous sex. He shouldn't feel guilty for that. That said, one more date wouldn't be too much to ask. If it didn't work out, she could at least say she had taken a real shot at trying to recapture the magic.

"Okay." She relented. "We can try another date. *One* more. And we'll see how it goes. A trip to Dallas sounds like an all-day affair, though. I won't be able to get away until next Wednesday when the trucks are closed."

Sebastian's brows knit together in confusion. "Don't you have staff that can handle things?"

"Yes..." But she wasn't the kind to leave her metal-and-rubber babies without supervision.

"You took last Saturday night off. I think you can do it again."

Lauren sighed. "I'll talk to my team and see what I can do." She supposed everything did go fine last weekend with the trucks. Amy and Javier were competent sous chefs. She just wasn't great at relinquishing control. That was why Amy had entered her in the contest to begin with.

"Great." Sebastian leaned in, his eyes asking the question she wasn't prepared to answer yet. But she didn't pull away. She let it happen, closing her eyes as his lips met hers. It was a brief kiss. A soft, gentle kiss. But a kiss completely unlike any of the ones they'd shared Saturday night.

She'd let the kiss happen in the hopes that it would spark something between them. That perhaps their bodies would finally remember what they'd shared and the fires would light in her belly again.

Nothing.

When he finally pulled away, Lauren noted a

flicker of disappointment and frustration in his green eyes. She knew exactly how he felt. They could both tell something was off, but neither of them knew what to do about it. Maybe a casual day in Dallas would make the difference.

She hoped so.

"Good night, Lauren." Sebastian raised his hand in parting and walked back to his BMW.

She watched him drive away before closing and locking her door. Stepping inside, Lauren kicked out of her heels in disgust. She walked over to her junk drawer on the kitchen island, where she kept a collection of pens, batteries, loose change and hair ties. Without hesitation, she swept the shoulder-length strands of her hair back off her face and into its usual bun on the top of her head. It looked nice down with the new highlights, at least her stylist had said so, but it just got in her way. She was pretty sure she got some butternut squash soup in it earlier. Sexy.

With it out of the way, she went over to her Sub-Zero refrigerator and removed a bottle of her favorite sparkling water. Then she pulled out a stool and sat at the large quartz island to think. The kitchen, and this kitchen in particular, was her happy place. There was something soothing about the stainless steel appliances, the cool stone countertops and the sleek white cabinets that calmed her nerves and cleared her mind. She wasn't remotely hungry, but she thought about getting up and cooking something.

After a moment of resting her toes, Lauren got up and unzipped the shift dress she'd worn to dinner. She let it slink into a puddle at her feet and stepped out, leaving it there. In her bra and panties, she went to the pantry and pulled out an apron. She returned to the island a moment later with an armful of vegetables and set to work cleaning and chopping.

It would become either soup or a frittata in the morning, she hadn't decided yet. But for now, she would chop.

The therapeutic rhythm pounded through her brain and when the last pepper was obliterated, she set down her knife and took a deep breath.

She never should've sought out Sebastian Wingate. She knew that now. He was a perfectly nice guy, even more handsome than she imagined he would be under the mask. But that night at the club had been special. A once-in-a-lifetime kind of night. And in trying to locate him, in reaching out to him in real life without masks and the late-night haze of vodka, it just wasn't the same.

Lauren would go with him to Dallas. She would see it through because she'd said she would. But she needed to accept the fact that it would probably end there. She would never have another enchanting night in the arms of her masked suitor. She hadn't given much thought to what a physical relationship with Sebastian would be like, but she knew in her heart it wouldn't be anything like what they'd already shared.

The spell was broken. The stroke of midnight brought all that to an end. And now Cinderella and the lovely fantasy that came along with it had turned back into a big, old pumpkin and some mice.

"For someone who just got home from a date, you look positively miserable."

Sutton looked down at his watch and then back at his brother as he came through the front door and tugged loose his tie. "Then again, it's nine o'clock. Not a good sign to be home this early."

Sebastian frowned at him and shook his head. "Thanks for the blow-by-blow commentary on how badly my date went. I should've brought you along to narrate."

His brother dropped his keys onto the coffee table and flopped down on the couch beside Sutton, who had been watching a college football game. "Beer?" he offered.

"Hell yeah."

Sutton got up and grabbed two fresh beers from the kitchen. He popped the tops and carried them back into the living room. They both took a few sips and silently watched football until it went to a commercial break. Sutton took the opportunity to press his brother for information. “So what happened?”

Sebastian shook his head. “I wish I knew. On paper, it should be perfect. And yet, it’s nothing like before. If she didn’t show up on my doorstep insisting she was the woman I met before, I wouldn’t believe it.”

Sutton frowned. He and his brother hadn’t had many conversations of depth recently. Too much had been going on in their lives. But he’d obviously missed something major and he needed the pieces filled in. “Back up. Who is this woman again?”

“Her name is Lauren Roberts. She’s the owner and chef of the Street Eats food trucks that are usually parked around downtown.”

Sutton recognized the name. He’d even eaten at Street Eats a couple times. The food was really good and it was quick for when he was moving from one meeting to the next without time to sit down for a meal. “Where did you meet her?”

“Well, that’s not so simple. I met her at the masquerade ball. I *think*. Then she showed up a few days later to introduce herself and apologize for acting out of character that night. At first, I was ecstatic. Now…not so much.”

“I get the feeling you’re skimming over the important stuff. Go back to the party. What happened there?”

“What didn’t?” Sebastian said with a sigh. “I

don't know what it was. Something about that night was different. *She* was different. Beautiful and exotic looking. With our masks we could pretend to be other people. I got caught up in it."

"I know what you mean," he admitted. It hadn't felt like the typical club party. He'd met women at those things before. He'd danced the night away with them. He'd even left with one before. But it wasn't like this. She hadn't lingered in his mind the way Red had. "It had to be the masks."

Sebastian nodded. "You know that I'm not the kind to get caught up with a lady at something like that. But she was entrancing. Yet somehow familiar." He sighed. "I felt so comfortable around her, I guess I let my guard down…and touching her was almost a religious experience. I can't even describe it. We had an extraordinary connection. And then the party ended, she was gone and I thought she was out of my life for good."

Sutton's nose wrinkled at his brother's words. While they were twins, they rarely did anything alike. They were night and day. And yet, they seemed to have had very similar experiences at the masquerade ball.

"I felt like such a fool for letting her get away. No name," Sebastian lamented. "No way to contact her. I hadn't even seen her face without the mask on. I spent the nights after the party lying in bed beating myself up for how I handled things. Something good finally happens to me and I let her slip through my fingers."

"It was an honest mistake," Sutton said. He'd made the same one. His masked temptress had run out while he slept and he only had her mask to show for it. He'd held it in his hands as he sat on the edge of his bed thinking about what a fool he'd been. On the plus side, misery loved company. He and Sebastian could lament their stupidity together.

"Then she showed up on our doorstep and I thought I'd been given a second chance with the woman of my dreams."

"You mean she just showed up at the house one day?" Sutton had never been jealous of his brother before, but there was a first time for everything. He wished his mystery woman had tracked him down. Instead, she'd fled in the night without a trace.

"Yes. She said she saw my picture in the newspaper and realized who I was. Told me she had to talk to me because of the way everything happened. I was stunned to have her just drop in my lap like that, so I jumped at the chance and asked her out to dinner. And now here I am, sitting with you, wondering where it all went wrong."

"So it wasn't the same?"

Sebastian shrugged. "I don't know how to describe it. I mean, Lauren is lovely. She's pretty and smart and honestly, a fling with a masked woman could've ended much worse when identities were revealed. But it's not like it was that night. The electricity, the draw…it's gone. She's just a nice woman and nothing more. That's all I can say about it. There was no spark."

"That sucks."

"You could say that," Sebastian grumbled. "And I don't understand it. I can't stop thinking about the masked woman. I've even dreamed about her. She was everything I wanted, like a fantasy that stepped out of my head and onto the dance floor. But Lauren is just not the same woman. She said she wasn't quite acting herself that night, but I don't think you can fake chemistry like that. She says she is the woman from that night, but in my gut I know it just can't be true." He shoved a hand through his hair. "I wish she'd left behind a glass slipper I could try on her foot to prove her identity one way or another."

That's when a dull ache started to worry at Sutton's stomach. There were so many similarities to their stories and yet Sutton hadn't mentioned much about that night to his brother or anyone else. Maybe there was more to this than just an innocent fling. But what were the odds that both of them would have a night like that, then the woman would show up on their doorstep claiming to be the one Sebastian had been with?

He didn't like having such paranoid thoughts, but with everything going on with Wingate Enterprises, they couldn't be too careful. Maybe someone had hired a couple women to come to the party and seduce them for information.

"Tell me more about her. But focus on that night at the party, not your date tonight, since we're not certain they're one and the same. Describe her as though she were two different people."

Sebastian nodded and closed his eyes. "The woman at the party had dark brown hair and large, dark eyes. Her hair was up, but I could tell it was longer. She was wearing a black mask and a long, red dress—"

"Stop," Sutton said, holding up his hand. "Are you sure about all of that? She had brown eyes, a red dress and a black mask?"

Sebastian rolled his eyes at his brother. "Of course, I'm certain. She's been on my mind ever since that night. I couldn't forget what she looked like if I tried. Why are you giving me the third degree on her?"

Sutton took a deep breath and tried to gather his thoughts. "Well, because I had a very similar experience at the party. And it happened to be with a brown-eyed brunette in a red dress and a black mask."

"That's a weird fluke."

"Perhaps. But what if it was the same woman?"

Judging by the expression on his twin's face, he wasn't buying it. "No way. There had to be more than one woman in a red dress there that night."

"Yes, but everything else seems too coincidental. We both meet a mystery woman in red and have anonymous affairs at the party? Maybe me, but *you*? You never do things like that. It's like we were targeted."

"Are you suggesting that we both slept with the same woman that night? And that she did it on purpose?" Sebastian winced with disgust as he said the words. "That's not possible. And even if it were… why would she want to do that?"

"Why would someone want to set us up to get the family kicked off the board and all our assets frozen?" Sutton countered.

His brother sat back in his seat and took another long swig of beer. "You think it's all related somehow? That the woman at the party targeted us on purpose because of something to do with the drug charges?"

It seemed far-fetched. He knew that. But so was both of them being under the seductive spells of such similar women on the same night. "Maybe. I wouldn't put it past anyone, anymore. No place is safe, not even the club."

"But why? Whether it was one woman or two dressed similarly, what does sleeping with us both get them?"

That, Sutton wasn't sure about yet. But he'd piece it together eventually, just the way he'd eventually get to the bottom of who had framed them. "Maybe just to set us up for some scandalous photos. More bad press for the family could ruin what little positive public opinion we have left. Or maybe she was hoping to get some information about us. Did you talk about the family or business at all with her?"

"No," Sebastian insisted. "Nothing personal, really. You?"

"No. We took full advantage of our anonymity at the party. What about at dinner tonight?"

His twin shook his head again. "It was all fairly light subjects. Mostly small talk. I'm not even sure Lauren knows much about the family, much less that she's the mastermind of the whole plot. She's not a club member or involved in Royal society at all. She's an outsider to all of this."

"Or so she wants you to think."

"That just doesn't ring authentic to me," Sebastian insisted. "I think you've got too much time on your hands if you're thinking up evil plots."

"And yet she knew enough about you to show up at the house even though she wasn't supposed to know who you were?"

His brother shrugged. "She said she realized who I was when she saw a picture of me in the paper the next day."

Sutton got up from the couch and went out to the garage to find Sunday's paper in the recycling bin. There, he found a picture of his brother wearing his wolf mask and a caption with his name. He carried it back inside and tossed it into Sebastian's lap. "That part could be true enough."

Sebastian read over the paper and then put it on the coffee table. "All that article tells anyone is that I was at the party in a wolf mask. So were you. What of it? If she is the woman I was with, wouldn't seeing that picture be enough to inspire her to track me down?"

"I don't know. Maybe it's just my imagination making more of this than there really is. Perhaps she got carried away and had a fling with us both. Maybe two women were dressed similarly and I don't know enough about fashion to tell them apart. But I think at the very least we should have Miles do a background check on Lauren. Make sure there isn't more to this."

"That's not a bad idea. Just to make sure." A muscle ticked in Sebastian's jaw. "But the more we talk about it, the more I really think it's just a case of chemistry gone awry. We're going to go out again. Maybe things will finally click. I was going to take her up to Dallas."

Sutton packed away his conspiracy theories and decided to call it a night. His team was losing, and, even with the lack of chemistry on Sebastian's date, he wouldn't be able to hide his jealousy of his brother for long. If it wasn't all a setup, then fate had brought Sebastian his mystery woman, but not his.

He made noises about being tired and went up

to his suite. There, he flopped down onto his bed and stared up at the ceiling for a moment. Then he rolled over and opened the bedside stand to pull out the black mask Red had left behind.

Sutton turned it over in his hands the way he had every night since the party. When he looked at it, he could see her beautiful brown eyes looking back at him. Those eyes had been so trusting. So open.

He didn't want to believe those same trusting eyes had an agenda and were just using him. He didn't want that night's memory to be tainted. It was his escape from the other problems in his life, not a part of them.

In that moment, he made a decision. If Red wasn't going to track him down, then he was going to find her. Whether she was Lauren Roberts or a spy or some other person entirely, he was going to get to the bottom of it all.

Five

Sutton studied the list his sister Beth had given him. On it was every single person that bought or was given tickets to the gala. On his computer, he'd filtered out all the men and the women that had come with their husbands. He'd like to think a married woman couldn't spend the whole night with him without her husband noticing. By the time he'd discarded family and all the women he knew from the club, he was left with a list of about ten women's names.

One of which was Lauren Roberts.

He considered giving the list to Miles when he asked for the background check on Ms. Roberts.

A little digging could help him pinpoint which, if any of them, might be the woman he met that night. Of course, he wasn't sure how he'd explain to his younger brother that he wanted him to weed out any women without brown hair and eyes from the list. That would prompt a lot of questions he didn't want to answer. How could he explain that he was obsessed with a woman but didn't know who she was? Or that he couldn't be sure she wasn't some spy sent to help ruin the family?

No. He'd have Miles run the check for Sebastian, but he would keep the rest of the list to himself for now. Decision made, he sent the filtered list to his printer and looked over it again once he could hold it in his hands. One of these women was the one he was looking for. He knew it. His heart hammered in his chest as he read the list again and again. He was so close to finding her.

"I've got an idea."

Sutton set aside the papers he was going through and looked at his brother, who had arrived suddenly in the doorway of their shared office. "Dare I ask?"

Sebastian came inside and settled down onto the overstuffed chair they'd moved in a few days before. "I told you that there's something wrong about Lauren that I can't put my finger on."

"Yeah." That was one way of saying it, although it was a lot more complicated than that.

"Well, I think I know what we should do to help

us figure it all out. I think you should be the one to go on the date with her."

That wasn't what Sutton was expecting to hear. "Go on a date with her? I thought you were going to say something practical like 'have her investigated,' which I'm already doing. I emailed Miles this morning with her information."

"Good. While he's doing that, it can't hurt for you to go out with Lauren."

Sutton furrowed his brow in confusion. "I don't understand. You mean you want me to go on the trip to Dallas you have planned for Saturday?"

"Exactly. She and I don't have the chemistry we did before and I know in my gut she isn't the one I spent the evening with. If you go and you two have chemistry, maybe that will help us get to the bottom of what's going on. Maybe she's your mystery gal in red, not mine, but we won't know until you meet her."

"You said she seemed very confident that you were the man she was looking for. She even went to the trouble of tracking you down at our rental house."

"Yes," Sebastian agreed, "but only because she saw my picture in the paper. But in that picture, I'm wearing my wolf mask."

"So?"

"So…you and I ordered the same mask, remember. What if she just presumed I was the person she spent the night with because I was wearing the wolf mask, too."

That was an intriguing thought. Twins in the same masks could confuse anybody that didn't know them well enough. Or at all, like Lauren. "Perhaps she was confused and didn't realize there were two of us in those masks. But don't you think she's going to wonder why I'm taking her out instead of you?"

Sebastian rolled his eyes. "Are you serious?"

"What?"

"I meant that you should go on the date, but as *me*, not as you. She won't know the difference and it will give you a chance to spend time with her one-on-one. Be Sebastian for the day and see what happens."

Coming from the brother that normally eschewed his twin-swapping shenanigans, Sutton was stunned. "That's an awfully big risk to take just because you have a hunch. What if she can tell the difference between us?"

"Come on, bro. Our own family and friends struggle with telling us apart. Do you really think a woman that's seen me twice without a mask would do any better?"

It was an interesting proposition, but one that was completely risk free for Sebastian. But he, on the other hand, was the one that would be stuck all day in another city with Lauren if things went wrong. Then again, she was on the short list of single women at the party. What if his brother was right and she was the one he'd spent the evening with?

"Counter-proposal," he murmured after a few minutes of consideration. "Let's test the waters first and see if I can pull this off. It's been a long time since I've pretended to be you to mess with people." Sutton reached for his phone and pulled up Lauren Roberts's Street Eats account on Instagram. Her trucks moved around each day, so you had to go online and see where they would be on a given day.

He started to look at the most recent post, but another caught his eye. It was a professional shot of a dark-haired woman with dark brown eyes. Her hair was up in a bun and she was wearing a white chef's coat. It was nothing close to the glamorous image of the woman in a red, beaded gown, but there was something about her that was just as striking. Maybe it was the bold confidence that he liked. Something about the pout of her lips and the heart-shape of her face seemed familiar, too. He tore his gaze away from the photo to read the description. It was the Street Eats owner and executive chef, Lauren Roberts herself.

Sebastian might just be right. This could be the woman Sutton had spent the most incredible night of his life with. There was something about her that drew him in. He couldn't imagine his brother spending time with Lauren and not being intrigued by her knowing smirk and bewitching, dark gaze. He scrolled back up to the daily post to see where he could track her down today.

"It looks like she's going to have the original truck at the Courtyard Shops, and Street Eats 2 will be at Royal Memorial Hospital today. What if I take your car into town under the guise of being you and pay her a little visit?" He tried not to suddenly sound too eager about his brother's idea, but his pulse was racing at the chance to potentially track down his mystery woman.

"If she doesn't suspect anything," he continued, "then I'll see if I can pull off a whole date this weekend as you. Hopefully, by that time, we'll get the information back from Miles and we'll have an idea if she's someone that can be trusted or not."

Sebastian grinned. "Brilliant. How do you know which truck she'll be at today?"

Sutton looked over the account. "Seems like she's always with her original truck based on what I see here, so I'll start there first."

"Excellent idea." Sebastian fished his car keys out of his pocket and tossed them over to his brother. "Don't scratch my baby."

Sutton rolled his eyes. He was the car aficionado. The car he'd just been forced to sell was worth three times what Sebastian's BMW would run. "Don't worry. I'm pretending to be you, so I'll drive like an old man."

"Ha, ha!" Sebastian retorted as he got up and left the room. "Good luck pretending to be as charismatic and suave as I am," he said over his shoulder as he disappeared down the hallway.

What a joke, Sutton thought to himself. Sebastian and he were alike in some ways, but polar opposites in others, especially when it came to the ladies. He loved his twin, but he was so uptight he squeaked. It didn't surprise him that any chemistry he might have with a mystery woman would be snuffed out by reality. Sebastian's dating habits were enough to put Sutton to sleep.

Over the years, his brother had brought around a long parade of sweet, southern debutantes that Mother would approve of. Not once had Sutton ever looked at one of his brother's girlfriends with the slightest bit of interest. He had a completely different taste in women from his twin. That alone should've been enough to convince him that there were two women in similar red dresses at the party that night. There's no way he and Sebastian would both be taken with the same woman, even if she was playing them both somehow.

Which meant that if Lauren Roberts wasn't Sebastian's girl, perhaps his brother was right and the pretty chef was *his* mystery lady. There was only one way to find out. He glanced down at his phone and noted the menu available for today.

"Tamales," he said with a satisfied grin. It kept getting better. No matter what, the trip wouldn't be a total loss because one of his favorites was on the menu.

Lauren was swamped. Tamales were always one of the more popular items at her food trucks. They sold well and they were assembled ahead of time, so it made for a less stressful day. She would do them more often, honestly, but she didn't want to get pigeonholed into one type of cuisine. There was a whole culinary palate out there in the world and she wanted to cook and taste it all.

They'd made it through lunch to the afternoon lull. Between about two and five, the crowds dropped down enough for them to reevaluate supplies, do additional food prep and if the site wasn't doing that well, to move to another spot.

Fortunately, she'd chosen a good place near the Courtyard Shops today. Priceless, the antique shop in the old barn, always seemed to do good business, as did Natalie Valentine's bridal salon. People said this time of year was the start of proposal season and it looked to be true. There were more than a few crowds of ladies heading into the store to try on gowns with their families and girlfriends.

Wedding gowns were of little interest to Lauren,

she could barely get through a successful first date, but she actually planned to head over to the artisan cheese shop later to see what she could find.

Amy was loading another batch of assembled tamales into the steamer when Lauren looked out front and saw a black BMW pull up. It wasn't an uncommon car, but the moment she laid eyes on it, she knew who it was. Her heart kind of sank at the idea of having to face Sebastian again so soon. He was a nice, handsome man and came from a good family. And her mother's voice in her mind urged her not to screw it up. But whatever they'd shared that night had been smothered by reality. Pretending otherwise was a painful experience for her and she was a terrible liar.

Sorry, Mom.

"We've got a customer," Lauren said to Amy, turning away from the window to busy herself on the other side of the kitchen.

She dismissed her friend's sigh of irritation as Amy dropped what she was doing to greet the diner waiting for them.

"Lauren, it's for you. Sebastian Wingate has come to pay you a visit."

Damn. She was hoping he was just hungry, but no, he wanted to see her specifically. Lauren took a deep breath and pasted a smile onto her face before turning back around. Sebastian was standing patiently with a wider-than-usual grin on his face.

As she approached the counter, she couldn't help but feel that he looked a little different today. Perhaps he was in a good mood and it changed his whole demeanor. Or maybe he was having a good hair day. But whatever it was, it made him appear happier and more open than before. It made him more appealing to her in an unexpected way.

"Good afternoon, Sebastian," she said with a smile. "What are you doing out here at the Courtyard Shops?"

He held up his phone. "I heard there were going to be some excellent tamales served out here today."

Lauren couldn't keep from blushing at the compliment. She dismissed most people's comments—good or bad—on her appearance, her intelligence even her sense of humor. But when folks spoke about her food, she knew it was genuine enough and she took it to heart. Those were the opinions that mattered the most to her. "That's sweet of you to say. You came all the way over here just for my tamales? The other truck is over by the hospital, which is a lot closer to your place."

"I really love tamales. But, of course, I couldn't pass up on the chance to see you, too. It was worth the extra driving time."

He sounded like he meant it. And given their last conversation on her porch about the inevitable demise of this relationship, Lauren was confused. Had he forgotten her desire to throw in the towel?

Or was he determined to make the most of their last try? She appreciated his determination to make things work, but she wasn't sure it would be enough to salvage things between them.

She focused on the food because it was easier than the relationship stuff. "We've got a fresh batch that will be ready in a few minutes if you'd like to wait."

"Sure. I don't mind."

"I've got things handled in here," Amy said loudly from over Lauren's shoulder. "Why don't you two go sit somewhere and I'll bring an order out to you when they're ready?"

Lauren snapped her head around and eyed her employee warily. Amy smiled sheepishly. She knew full well how things were faring with Sebastian, but she was pushing anyway. And she would get away with it, because he had heard her and it would be impolite for Lauren to turn her offer down.

"That would be great," she said between gritted teeth. Turning back to Sebastian, she asked, "Would you like a drink to go with your tamale?"

"Sweet tea?"

"You bet."

Lauren poured them both glasses and gave Amy a cutting glance before walking to the back of the truck. When she opened the door, Sebastian was waiting there for her, his hand extended to help her down. She thrust a glass into his hand instead and got down using the handle on the door the way she always did.

Earlier that morning, the truck had set up an umbrella and a portable picnic table to give an option to anyone who wanted to sit and eat. Downtown that wasn't an option, but here they had more space and the owners didn't mind. Lauren gestured over to the empty table she'd wiped down not long before he arrived.

They both settled in sitting across from one another. For some reason, Lauren felt the flutter of butterflies in her stomach. Perhaps it was the way Sebastian was looking at her. There was a new curiosity there, but underlying it, was an unexpected dose of heat. He seemed to appreciate the way she looked today, which made no sense at all. She'd looked ten times better at the party and even when they went out to dinner. Today she was dressed to cook, with her hair in a tight bun and a boxy chef's coat over her T-shirt and jeans.

His silence was just as unnerving as his heavy appraisal of her. He didn't try to make any small talk like he had before. He just sipped his tea and watched her.

Lauren had to break the silence. "I wasn't expecting to see you today. Or at all until Saturday."

"I know. It was a spur-of-the-moment decision. I saw your post on my Instagram feed and decided I should come out. I haven't gotten to try your food yet, after all. If I'm dating a chef, I should get some of the perks, right?"

Lauren couldn't stop herself from returning his smile. "Honestly, most of the guys I've dated haven't seen it as a perk. It takes up too much of my time and doesn't leave much left over for them."

"It's not like you're just a chef at someone else's restaurant. You're running your own business and trying to build it up. That takes time, I know. Now, without a company to run, I don't know what to do with myself. I end up dropping in on pretty ladies with lame excuses about wanting lunch."

Lauren chuckled. "It wasn't a lame excuse. Just a transparent one."

Before she could ask Sebastian about how things were going with the Wingate investigation, Amy showed up with two paper trays of tamales and a spicy Bloody Mary rice she was trying out on the menu today. "Bon appétit," she said, wagging her eyebrows suggestively at Lauren before she turned back to the truck.

"Wow, this looks great," Sebastian said. He took his fork and immediately dove into his steamy hot food.

Lauren just waited for the reaction, holding her breath the whole time. She watched him blow on a bite before putting it in his mouth and chewing thoughtfully. He took a second bite before speaking, making her tenser with each second that ticked by.

Him liking her food was about more than just goodwill in their relationship. Positive word of mouth in his social circles could do wonders for her business, even if they didn't continue to see each other.

"This is without a doubt the best tamale I've ever had," he said at last.

A rush of air escaped from Lauren's lungs. "Really? You're not just saying that?"

"Not at all." He put another bite in his mouth and chewed happily. "So good."

Within minutes, his plate of food—and hers—were safely hidden away in Sebastian's belly. He had an appetite today she didn't remember from their dinner together. So either he really liked it or he was very hungry. He even made a bit of a mess of himself in the process.

Without thinking, she reached out with her napkin and wiped a bit of the chili sauce from the corner of his mouth. It was a weirdly familiar gesture for people in their position and his eyes met hers for a moment, as they both seemed to realize it at once.

Sebastian's hand shot up and caught hers. As his warm fingers enveloped her own, the napkin fell from her hand. Neither of them really noticed. All Lauren was aware of was the feel of his skin pressed against hers. Familiar. Addictive. Her heart started racing in her chest as though her body suddenly remembered his touch. Flashes of their night together, of these same big, masculine hands on her body, rushed to her mind all at once.

And just like that, their chemistry was back in full force. Like a lightning bolt had struck them through the conduit of the aluminum umbrella, it hit Lauren all at once. She wasn't sure what had changed, but things were definitely different today.

Sebastian noticed it, too. His green eyes narrowed at her, suddenly more wary, yet more interested than they had been since she'd shown up on his doorstep. With his gaze fixed on her, he unconsciously licked his lips. Then he brought his hand down to where he could look at her fingertips and took a deep breath. "Your manicure has held up nicely."

That wasn't what she expected him to say. Especially since Sebastian hadn't mentioned her nails before. He might have commented about them at the club, but not since then. It seemed odd that he would mention them now. Of course, maybe he was just searching for something to say to break up the tension crackling between them.

"I'm surprised they've done so well," she said. "Cooking is hard work on hands. They usually don't look so polished. That's a remnant of my makeover."

"Makeover?"

Lauren frowned. If she wasn't looking Sebastian dead in the face, she would think she was talking to someone else today. "Yeah, you know. I told you about how I won the party tickets and makeover as part of that contest on the radio."

A moment of realization flickered in his eyes for a moment and then vanished as he smiled again. "Oh, yes. I'd forgotten about that. Well, they did a great job. You look just as lovely today. Just put on that red gown and we could be back at the club playing billiards."

Lauren froze for a moment, gently extracting her hand from his. That was the first time he'd made any real reference to their night together. At first, she'd thought he was just being gentlemanly about it. If they were trying to start over in their relationship, not talking about their hot one-night stand on a pool table was advisable.

But at the same time, there'd been no mention of their evening together at all. He didn't seem to remember that she liked dirty martinis despite buying her several that night. None of their conversations in the alcove of the club or out on the dance floor seemed familiar to him. She'd chalked it up to drinking too much.

And now, suddenly a pool table reference of all things. A complete one-eighty. When she looked up at him in surprise, there was a knowing heat in his gaze. It was enough to make her cheeks flame with embarrassment, and this time she had no mask to hide behind.

"You're not very good at camouflaging what you're thinking. Your face is very expressive. I know I may have said this before, but I like being able to see your whole face. I feel like with your mask on I was missing out on so many facets of your emotions and expressions."

He hadn't mentioned it before. Like everything else that night, he'd done a complete reset until this very moment. Lauren was both extremely confused and intrigued. Whatever initial disappointment she'd felt about meeting her masked man in real life had suddenly gone out the window.

"Like right now," he continued, "if you had that mask on I wouldn't see those cute little lines between your eyebrows that pop up when you're thinking. I only ever got your eyes. Brown and gold, looking right through me somehow, even behind my own mask. I like having the whole picture."

Lauren was stunned by his words. What could she say to something like that? He suddenly seemed to notice and remember every detail about her. Most people didn't pay any attention to the golden starbursts in her eyes, much less speak about them as though he'd memorized every honeyed fleck. Her heart stuttered in her chest as warmth flooded her cheeks.

"I need to get back to the truck," she said instead. "But we're still on for Saturday, right?"

"Absolutely."

"Do you have plans for what we're going to do in Dallas yet?"

"Not exactly. But there's a pop-up restaurant that I've read about that's going to be operating that day. I thought that might appeal to the chef in you. Maybe give you some ideas for your own business. Would you like me to call and get reservations?"

Lauren had thought a lot about trying out a pop-up shop. It would let her dip her toe into the waters of having a permanent restaurant and see how it went. She even had her eye on an empty location on the square that would be perfect. "That sounds great. And don't you have an aunt in the area?"

"My aunt Piper, yes."

"I'd love to see her gallery if we have time while we're up there. I've wanted to go but never have found the time to do it."

A stiffness returned to Sebastian's expression that reminded her more of her tense dinner date than her billiards partner. Apparently he could switch between those sides of himself like flipping a coin. "Sure," he said without much enthusiasm. "I'll see what I can do."

Six

Being with Lauren was easy. Lying to her and pretending to be his brother was not.

Sutton hated doing this. It felt all wrong. He was constantly walking on eggshells hoping he wouldn't say something that would give him away. So far Lauren didn't seem to notice. Or at least, she didn't seem to mind the change. She'd noted that he seemed more relaxed. That made sense. Even Sutton at his most tense wasn't anywhere near as uptight as Sebastian was on a random Tuesday.

Since he hadn't managed to screw things up, he'd picked her up in his brother's BMW and they drove up to Dallas together. While the ride itself was outwardly pleasant, he had a hard time keeping his hands on the wheel. Being trapped in the same small space with her, her scent lingering in the air… He desperately wanted to pull the car over and kiss her until he was gasping for air. But he kept his hands on the wheel and his mouth to himself.

He wasn't sure why his brother didn't see much in Lauren, but Sutton certainly did. She wasn't stunningly beautiful like so many of the debutantes that had circled around the twins since their teen years. He was pretty certain that was only because she didn't put in the hours of effort on her appearance like they had. That said, he was able to appreciate a natural beauty in Lauren that he hadn't really been exposed to before.

Things like her flawless porcelain skin. It wasn't from perfectly-applied foundation, her skin just looked that good. Furthermore, her thick, dark lashes didn't require mascara, her arched brows didn't need to be penciled in and her lips were pink and full without lipstick, liner or gloss. Yes, she'd enhanced all those things that night at the ball, but he found her just as attractive, if not more so, when she was working in her food truck and doing what she loved.

And if his attraction to her wasn't enough, the minute he touched her, any doubts about her true identity went out the window. She was the woman he spent the night with at the club. There was an instantly familiar chemistry. The catch of her breath when he caught her wrist, the widening of those brown-and-gold eyes as she felt the same electric current running between them… He knew it all by heart.

That woman had been by his side from minutes after his arrival until she slipped out late in the night, leaving her mask behind. That meant she had little time to acquire a new mark and seduce his brother, as well. And based on their discussions, Lauren had no idea Sebastian Wingate had a twin brother, or knew much of anything else about his family. Bottom line? She wasn't likely a spy sent to take down the family with that little information. But she could still be playing him, so to be safe, he intended to keep his distance until he got the report back on Lauren from his brother Miles.

That made the distance to Dallas a painful exercise in self-restraint for Sutton. It actually made him wish he hadn't chosen to wear his tightest pair of jeans for the date.

"So are we going to the gallery first, or to the pop-up?" Lauren asked after a few miles of nothing but the radio murmuring softly in the background.

"The gallery is up first. I checked the hours and it won't be open that late, so I wanted us to have as much time as you wanted to there. Our reservations at the restaurant are for later."

To be honest, Sutton was not excited about going

to the gallery. His aunt Piper was very observant and had an eye for detail. It made her an excellent gallery owner and a very nosy aunt. If anyone had a chance of blowing his charade as Sebastian, it was Piper. But avoiding the gallery would raise flags, too. So all he could do was go to the gallery as requested and hope for the best.

Rounding the corner near his aunt's place, Sutton pulled into a spot along the street. He helped Lauren out of the car and escorted her down the sidewalk and into the gallery.

He loved Piper's gallery and he could tell that Lauren was instantly taken with it, as well. It had stark white walls with colorful pieces every direction you looked. Paintings, sculptures and even a modern glass-and-metal mobile that hung from the ceiling, brought the space to life.

"This," Lauren said with conviction, "is what I want."

"You want an art gallery?" Sutton asked.

"No. But the feel. The colors. The modern lines. One day if I get to open my own restaurant, I want it to look like this. I love it."

"Well, I'm sure that Aunt Piper would be happy to sell you a few pieces for the walls when you're ready."

Lauren chuckled dismissively. "I can't afford a restaurant without wheels. What makes you think I can afford to hang expensive art on the walls?"

Sutton shrugged. "Maybe she could consign them to you if they're too expensive. You could ask her about it. Some of the pieces are her own work, so she might also be willing to make you a deal. In addition to that, my aunt has an eye for young, talented artists and likes to showcase their work here for exposure. These pieces probably aren't as expensive as you'd think."

A petite woman dressed in all black approached them. Sutton didn't recognize her, and that was a relief. "Welcome to Holloway Gallery. Can I help you?" she asked.

"I'm Sebastian Wingate, Piper's nephew." Sutton focused very hard on his words to say the right name. "I brought a friend up to see her place for the first time. Is she here today?"

"No, actually she's out of town," the woman said. "She won't be back until Monday, but feel free to walk around and let me know if you need anything."

He nodded, trying to hide his relief, and the gallery employee disappeared. With the worry of exposure out of the way, he could focus on enjoying himself. Lauren's eye drew her to a large, colorful portrait and he followed her there. They made their way through the gallery, discussing pieces and talking about which ones would look best in her future restaurant. So far, his vote was for a pop art piece of a giant avocado.

They were admiring a painting on the far wall

when the front door's bell chimed. Sutton turned around to find someone he knew stepping into the gallery. "Brian?"

The man turned around to look in Sutton's direction and recognition lit up his face. "Hey," he said as he walked toward them, carefully avoiding names and indicating to Sutton that he didn't know which one of the twins he was talking to.

Perfect.

"Sebastian," he said knowingly, and Brian sighed in relief. "And this is my friend, Lauren Roberts. Lauren, this is Brian Cooper. Although we're technically not family, he's like a cousin because he's the nephew of the man we all call Uncle Keith. Keith was my father's best friend and he's basically been at my mother's side since my father had his stroke and then passed away."

Sutton wouldn't elaborate on the creepy turn "Uncle" Keith's attention to his mother had taken since his father died. He didn't actually care for the man. But his mother seemed happy enough with him around, so he'd decided it wasn't any of his business. Others in the family were less welcoming to Keith's attentions to Ava.

Lauren smiled politely and shook Brian's hand. Sutton couldn't help but notice that Brian seemed disinterested in talking to them. At the very least, distracted. He kept glancing over Sutton's shoulder to the gallery behind him, as though he were looking for something or someone.

"Brian is an attorney here in Dallas," Sutton explained to Lauren. "So what are you doing up here at the gallery?" Sutton asked. "Looking for a piece to hang in your firm's lobby?"

"No, although that isn't a bad idea. I was hoping to have a word with Piper."

Sutton couldn't fathom what Keith's nephew would have to say to his aunt, but he didn't press the issue. Instead, he delivered the bad news. "We just spoke to the lady here and she said Piper won't be back until Monday."

Brian frowned, but nodded in acceptance. "I guess I should've called before I came all the way down here. Not a total waste of an afternoon, though. I got to see you and this lovely lady. What are you two doing in Dallas?"

"We just drove up for the day and thought we'd stop in to see the gallery."

"What else do you have planned?"

"After this, maybe some walking around downtown before our dinner reservation. We're checking out a pop-up restaurant tonight."

"That sounds fun. Well, I'll let you two continue with your afternoon. It was good to see you." Brian backed away toward the door and waved his hand in parting.

"You, too," Sutton said as the family friend

slipped out the door. "That was weird," he murmured aloud once the door closed.

"Why is that?" Lauren asked.

Sutton just shook his head. "Don't worry about it. Are you done here? What do you say we go get some ice cream and walk around for a bit? The weather is nice enough."

"Sounds good." Lauren grabbed one of the gallery's business cards off the counter as they went to the door. "Just in case I get a place someday," she said before stuffing it into her pocket.

Sutton didn't know Lauren very well, but he was confident she'd need that card sooner than later.

Lauren had never been to a pop-up restaurant before. It was a relatively new concept—at least to her—and she was anxious to see how it worked. After Sebastian mentioned coming here, she'd looked up more about the restaurant online. Like hers, it operated primarily as a food truck. One Saturday a month, it would pop-up in a different brick-and-mortar location. Sometimes in vacant venues. Other times in operational restaurants looking to take a night off. And sometimes under a tent in an old K-Mart parking lot. This had helped the restaurant build a large, cult following and they were hoping to open a permanent location within the year.

It was an intriguing idea to Lauren. There wasn't a lot of unused real estate in Royal, Texas, but there were some options. She just had to convince the property owner to let her do it. Oh, and find a way to come up with everything she needed for a fully functioning restaurant.

As they walked in the front door, she quickly realized her dream was really just a far-fetched fantasy. This was more than just a restaurant squatting in an old retail space. They had completely taken over the site and if you didn't know what you were walking into, you might think this was their permanent location. That cost money.

Money Lauren didn't have. She wasn't the local lottery-winning celebrity. And all her extra cash went into keeping the trucks running.

This restaurant was experienced and had spared no expense with their design and implementation. The stark black-and-white theme carried through the space, punctuated by dark red roses in bud vases on each table. White fabric draped the walls, Edison lights hung overhead and black-and-white photography was placed with care every direction you looked. Two dozen black tables with pressed white linen filled the space, surrounded by chairs they probably rented each time from a party supply company.

Soft music played from speakers overhead and a golden light twinkled from the votive candles on each dinner table. The scent of roses and the candles lingered in the room along with the spicy and enticing scents of garlic, onion and simmering tomato sauce.

She loved Italian food and she was excited to find out what was on Mama's Secrets menu tonight. Normally the food truck offered classic handheld favorites like meatball subs, chicken parmesan hoagies and fried arancini balls described as being the size of a regulation softball. Tonight, their website promised the same great tastes fans loved, but utensils would be required for a change.

Judging by the crowds, their dedicated customers had shown up in full force. While Sebastian checked in, Lauren noticed that every table was full but one and a few people were lingering around the doorway, awaiting their turn. That was good. Better people waiting for tables than tables waiting for people, she'd been told once by a wise mentor.

Luckily, their reservation put them ahead of the crowd. The one corner table that was unoccupied had been waiting for them. Sebastian placed his hand on Lauren's lower back and guided her ahead of him to follow the hostess to their seats.

It was the first time he'd touched her—really touched her—today. He'd taken her hand to help her out of the car, but otherwise, he'd been very hands-off. Considering that Lauren's nervous system was humming with excitement every time he got close, it was extremely frustrating. She almost hated to pull away from the heat of his hand to take her seat, but she couldn't keep the hostess waiting.

Seated together, they both lifted the sheet of paper that served as the day's menu. Lauren's mouth was watering as she looked over the options. Osso bucco with risotto. Veal saltimbocca with a polenta cake. Cacio e Pepe pasta. Eggplant parmesan. Potato gnocchi with pork shoulder. There were so many amazing sounding options to choose from, she hardly knew what to pick.

Adding to her indecision was the distraction across the table. Lifting her gaze from the paper, she noticed Sebastian was watching her again. This new habit of his was unnerving. He'd never done it before the day at the food truck. Now, every time she looked up, he was watching her. Appraising her somehow. There was a hunger in his eyes that had nothing to do with Italian food. And yet, he kept his distance.

He hadn't kept his distance that night at the club. He couldn't keep his hands off of her. What had changed, aside from the masks? Sebastian said he preferred seeing her without it, but his actions said otherwise. He seemed conflicted, both wanting her and distancing himself. It made all her insecurities flare up uncomfortably, sending the tasty menu items to the back of her mind.

"Have you decided?" she asked. He wasn't looking at his menu, so it seemed a reasonable question.

"I thought I'd let you order for me. You're the chef that knows all about food. I'll let you pick."

Lauren's lips parted, ready to argue, but she stopped. If he wanted her to order, she would. No one had ever asked her to before, and this gave her the opportunity to show off her foodie knowledge. "Okay. Well, if there were two of me at this table, we would have the arancini, the gnocchi and I think…the osso bucco. Hopefully there will be room left for tiramisu."

Sebastian laughed. It was a hearty and familiar sound, but not one she'd heard lately. It vibrated to her core, and released some of the tension she'd been holding in her shoulders. He'd been so serious when she first approached him. Perhaps he'd finally loosened up around her. His idea to leave town for a more casual date was a good idea, looking back at it.

When the waiter arrived, she ordered it all, adding a plate of fried squash blossoms for good measure and a bottle of red wine to compliment it all nicely.

"You're going to have to roll me back to Royal," he said. "Are we going to be able to eat all that? I expect you to hold up your side of this."

"With pleasure."

He nodded with visible appreciation. "I'd like to see that. I'm so used to women pulling the usual girl trick and barely eating on the date. I know they're hungry. I can hear their stomach rumbling while they pick at their salad. I figure when they get home they raid their refrigerators. But offer them a buttered roll and they'll practically stab you with their unused steak knife."

"I'm a chef. Food is life. I'm always eating." It wasn't a pretty statement. Or the kind of thing most women would say to a man on a date, but it was true. To drive the point home, she tore off a piece of the focaccia bread the waiter had put on the table and dipped it in oil and herbs. "And I'm not scared of bread," she added before taking a bite.

"I like it." He took a piece of bread for himself. "So how do you stay so slender if you aren't pathologically afraid of carbs?"

She hardly thought of herself as slender, but she would accept the compliment. "Stress, for one thing. I'm on my feet for hours in the trucks. When the trucks aren't open, I'm shopping, prepping, catching up the books and inventories. My pedometer tops twenty thousand steps most days. I also have an elliptical I try to get on regularly to get my heart rate up and burn off the day's overindulgences." She raised up the glass of red wine she'd chosen. "Like this. After all this Italian food, I will have to do an hour when I get home or in the morning for sure."

"I sit at a desk all day," he admitted. "Or I did practically from college graduation until now. Now I just sit around the house at a loss of what to do with myself. I used to swim, but the pool was taken with the family home. I play golf or tennis from time to time, but it's not enough to really count. Thankfully, a good metabolism seems to run in my family. We're all fairly slim."

"Lucky. I have to work at it, but it helps that I'm also incredibly picky when it comes to food. I'll eat almost every fruit, vegetable, grain and meat known to man, but if I don't care for the way it was prepared, I'll spit it out and waste the calories on something better. Processed, canned boxed junk usually isn't worth it to me. I grew up on that stuff and now I can't stand it. But give me a beautiful slice of imported cheese, some crusty artisan bread, some ripe fruit and good wine, and I'll eat every last crumb without fail."

Sebastian smiled another wide, genuine smile. She was getting used to seeing those out of the more-relaxed version of him. "I like it. You cook and you eat. You're beautiful. Smart. Sexy." He reached out for her hand and ran his thumb over the back of it before bringing it to his lips. He pressed his mouth to her skin, his gaze never leaving hers. "And you're dating me." He seemed surprised somehow by that fact.

Lauren's mouth fell open and she nearly groaned aloud at the feel of his lips against her skin. She managed a nervous laugh and pulled her hand away while she still had the willpower to do it. "I-I don't get it," she stuttered. "You flatter me while piling on yourself. Why wouldn't I be interested in you?"

He sighed and sat back to take a large sip of his wine. "This isn't exactly the greatest year of my life. Things are different now, but there was a time where I was downright arrogant. Cocky, even. Women were lucky to catch my eye and more than once I've had women fight over me. The Wingate boys have always been a hot commodity in Royal."

"You have a brother?" she asked.

Sebastian seemed to stiffen in his seat for some reason. "Yes," he said. "I have a younger brother, Miles. He's off the market now, however. He's lucky to have found Chloe. Now he doesn't have to look at a woman and see that look in their eyes."

Lauren flinched. "What look is that?"

"Like I'm tainted somehow. I don't know how closely you've followed what's going on with my family, but it's not good. I've gone from the CF—*I mean CEO* of my family business and living on a huge estate to losing everything. My job, the company, our family home… It's all gone. I'm not sure we'll ever fully recover. At this point, I'm going to be lucky not to end up in an orange jumpsuit."

She hadn't realized their situation was as dire as all that. No wonder he was so serious and uptight when she showed up at his door. She wasn't sure she'd be able to trust anyone if she were in a mess like that. "Prison? Wow. That is serious stuff. I've heard a little bit, but I haven't paid much attention to it all. I'm usually too busy to focus on town gossip."

His jaw tightened as he nodded. "Are you going to look at me that way, now?"

There was the slightest flicker of vulnerability in his green eyes as he asked the question. Everyone must have turned their backs on Sebastian and his family. It made her heart ache to think of that. But she understood how it felt. She'd never been truly accepted by the elites in this town. Most of them ignored her and the ones that didn't were downright cruel. She only fit in when she was wearing a mask. Her dreams of having a successful, high-end restaurant in Royal were just that. Dreams. Unless she could find a way to make them love her food enough to overlook her lack of social pedigree.

She was a great chef, but she wasn't a miracle worker.

Lauren looked him straight in the eye. She was known for being brutally honest, although it usually involved food critiques. She wouldn't lie to boost his ego, but he would have to be honest with her, too. "Are you guilty of anything you and your family are being accused of?"

"No," he said sharply, and his spine straightened defiantly as he spoke. Every inch of his body suddenly seemed to tighten with the audacity of the allegations. "Someone has gone out of their way to ruin us all and I don't know why."

"I believe you," she said softly. And she did. She didn't know much about Sebastian, but she trusted the man sitting across the table from her. Maybe she shouldn't, she had a bad habit of being too naïve when it came to men, but she did. "Then no, I won't look at you like you're tainted. As long as you give me the same courtesy."

"Of course. Why would I look at you that way?" He seemed genuinely surprised by her stipulation.

Apparently the tale of the infamous school dance at the club hadn't reached him. He was older and perhaps hadn't heard about Dunk Tank, or at least didn't realize Lauren was one and the same. He didn't see her as an outcast or an interloper into his world. She was grateful for that. He was one of the few that saw her just as she was.

Out of the corner of her eye, she spotted the waiter coming with the arancini and squash blossoms. The perfect way to end the current line of conversation.

"No reason," she said with a dismissive smile. "I hope you're hungry."

Seven

Sutton had never been so elated to read a piece of paper in his whole life. He supposed he could only be more relieved to read the charges against his family were dropped. But since that wasn't likely to happen, he would be happy enough with this.

Lauren Roberts's background check came back sparkly clean. Miles had gone above and beyond researching her and hadn't come up with anything questionable. She had no contacts with their company or competitors. Nor had she received any large payments from a mysterious source. Which proved she wasn't a spy or out to ruin his family, best anyone could tell.

It was a huge weight off his shoulders. He liked Lauren. A lot. He'd been enthralled by his mystery lover, but surprisingly enough, getting to know the woman behind the mask was just as exciting. If this background check had held adverse information about her, he would've been extremely disappointed.

But now that he knew for certain, he was faced with an ugly truth. He was the only liar in this relationship. Sebastian's suspicions were based on a lack of chemistry, but that hadn't been a problem for Sutton because Lauren was his masked lover. Sebastian's girl was still out there somewhere, so they had no real reason for switching places on Lauren.

It was time to come clean. And he would do it at dinner tonight. Not only because he had to, but because he wanted to. He told himself he couldn't seduce her while she thought he was Sebastian. But he wanted her. Badly. And the only way he could have her was to explain who he really was. And then, if she didn't hate him when he was done, maybe they could take their relationship to the next level.

It was a risky prospect, but he didn't have a choice if he wanted to see Lauren again. Simple as that.

Sutton made reservations that night at The Glass House. He knew Sebastian had already taken her there, but he was limited on options in Royal. Unless they wanted to go to the Silver Saddle Bar or the Royal Diner on Main Street, it was The Glass House or eating at the club. Lauren really should open a place here in town. Royal needed another great dining option and she was the perfect person to do it. If he wasn't in such a pinch, he'd bankroll it himself.

But considering all he really had left to his name was his white Audi R8 Coupe, he'd have to wait until all the crap with Wingate Industries blew over.

Tonight, he dressed like Sutton, not his brother. He chose his favorite gray suit and a navy silk shirt. No tie. He hated wearing ties. Then he fixed his hair in the messier style he preferred and wore his cologne of choice. It was a relief to finally step out the door as himself. Being his brother was frustrating and frankly—a little boring.

When he pulled up in front of Lauren's house, he watched her step outside with a wrinkle of confusion between her brows. He got out and opened the door for her to get inside.

"What happened to the BMW?" she asked. Then she turned to look at him. "And what happened to you?"

Sutton grinned. "I decided to let it all hang out tonight," he said. "I'll explain more at the restaurant."

She looked at him curiously, but got into the car without any more questions. "I'm surprised you suggested we go back to The Glass House," she remarked as they drove toward the Bellamy Hotel. "But then I noticed their seasonal menu has completely changed and I didn't mind so much. They've added a few amazing new dishes."

Lauren continued speaking with enthusiasm about the food and what she was going to order tonight. While Sutton appreciated the excitement that emanated from her when she talked about her passion for food, he barely heard a word she had to say. All he heard, all he could think about, were the worries in his own head. How would he tell her? When should he do it? Right away? Maybe wait until dessert? Was he only delaying the inevitable demise of this relationship?

Probably. But every moment he got to spend with Lauren was a gift. And she looked especially lovely tonight. She was wearing a sexy little black dress that clung to her delicious curves and showcased her shapely legs. It was like a sucker punch to the gut the moment she opened the door. And if she'd worn it alone, they might never have made it to the restaurant. But it was a cooler night, so he waited as she put on a demure cream sweater with shiny pearl buttons. It covered a lot of skin, but also drew his attention to her exposed collarbones, long neck and bare earlobes. He immediately wished he could buy her a strand of pearls and matching earrings to wear with that outfit. The old Sutton wouldn't have thought twice about making that purchase. He might even take a detour on the way to the restaurant to buy it on the spot at the local jewelry store.

But this Sutton just pasted on a smile, swallowed his irritation and walked her to his car. The situation with his family wouldn't last forever. And when they were vindicated and things went back to normal, he would buy her that necklace. Even if she wasn't speaking to him any longer.

"Sebastian?" Lauren asked after they'd been driving for a few minutes.

He snapped out of his thoughts, realizing that for now, he was still answering to his brother's name. "What?" he asked.

"I asked you what you thought about the red snapper."

"Fish isn't my favorite," he said.

"Didn't you get the grouper when we went there last time?"

Damn it. This charade needed to be over so he could stop worrying about every word that came out of his mouth. "I did. Grouper is fine. I just meant red snapper. I've always thought it smelled too fishy to me," he said, hoping that would patch his mistake for now.

"It's actually a very mild fish, a little nutty and almost sweet. You should try it."

"Maybe," he said, dismissing the conversation as they pulled into the hotel parking lot. Sutton opted to valet the car, tipping extra to keep it close.

He didn't need the valets going on a joyride in his baby. And once he told the truth, the date could end sooner than he expected. Might as well keep it on hand, just in case.

Once they were settled into the restaurant, food ordered and wine in hand, he decided it was time. He couldn't put this off anymore.

"Lauren, I need to talk to you about something."

Her eyes widened slightly as she set down her wineglass. "What is it?"

This was it. He just had to say the words out loud the way he'd practiced them in his head. "I told you the other night about how volatile the situation is with my family right now. Lately, we're not sure who we can really trust."

"That's reasonable," she murmured.

She was being too understanding. Normally that would help, but now it just made him feel worse about lying to her. He held up his hand before she said anything else that would make this harder. "When you came to the house that first day, it was because you thought you'd had a one-night stand with Sebastian Wingate. But you didn't."

Her gaze narrowed at him. "I don't understand."

"You saw the photo in the paper and assumed you'd been with Sebastian because of the mask. But there were two men at the party that night with the same mask. I was the other man."

She searched his face as though she were looking for the answers she needed, shaking her head. "What are you talking about? You *are* Sebastian Wingate."

Sutton took a deep breath. "I'm not. I'm his identical twin brother, Sutton. You've been going out with me while I pretended to be Sebastian, since I visited you at the food truck."

Her jaw dropped. He could almost see her running through the last week, thinking about all the signs she'd missed. Dread pooled in his gut, and he gave her a moment to process it all before he dared to say anything else.

"So, you're just like the others," she spat after the long silence.

That stopped him short. That wasn't what he expected her to say at all. "What others?" What was she talking about?

"All you rich snobs in Royal are the same. Do you just sit around your clubhouse, celebrating how much money you have and thinking of amusing ways to mess with people that don't fit in? Do you enjoy making them feel like you accept them into your little clique, then pull the rug out from under them just for fun?"

Where was this coming from? "No, Lauren." He reached across the table to take her hand. "Of course not. It isn't like that at all. We just weren't certain we could trust you."

"Trust *me*?" she said with her voice hovering on

the edge of hysteria. Her face had flushed red with anger and her eyes were glassy with unshed tears as she untangled her hand from his fingers. "You're the untrustworthy one, Sam. Steve. Whatever the hell you said your name is."

"Sutton," he repeated. "Please don't be upset. I can explain everything."

"I—" she hesitated "—I have to go." She pushed up from the table and tossed her napkin into her seat.

"At least let me take you home," he insisted. This hadn't gone the way he had hoped, but even if she never wanted to see him again, he still wanted to take her home. That was the least he could do.

"No, thank you. I'll call an Uber."

"Lauren, please." He reached out for her arm as she turned to leave.

"Don't touch me," she hissed with a fiery gaze. The tears were gone now, replaced with pure anger and betrayal. He'd never seen a look like that on her face and he never wanted to see it again. She jerked her arm from his grasp and spun to make for the exit.

Every eye in the restaurant was now on the two of them, so as much as he wanted to chase her out of the restaurant, he held up his hands in surrender and let her go. Instead, he could only watch as Lauren slipped through the tables to the door and disappeared into the Bellamy lobby.

He'd screwed up. Bad.

* * *

"What's wrong with you today?"

Lauren sighed, but didn't turn to face Amy. She'd been avoiding having this discussion with her all day, but now they were cleaning up at the end of the night and without any customers to distract them, Amy always got chattier. "Nothing is wrong. I'm just tired."

"I've seen you tired. This isn't tired. Did something happen with Sebastian?"

You could say that. And yet, not exactly. Nothing much had happened with Sebastian. But *everything* had happened with Sutton, who she hadn't even known existed until last night.

Identical twins. Really? When had her life become so melodramatic?

"Hey look, it's Gracie." Amy opened the window to the food truck and shouted out the window. "Gracie!"

Lauren turned to see Gracie Diaz walking down the sidewalk past the truck. But she didn't stop when Amy called out to her. That was odd. She opened the back of the truck to intercept her. "Gracie?"

She stopped short, looking at Lauren as though she wanted to escape instead of chat. "Um, hi, Lauren. I've got to go." She turned to start back down the sidewalk.

"Are you okay? Is something wrong?" Normally even if she wasn't hungry, she would pop in to say hello. They hadn't seen her in days, now. It wasn't like her at all.

Gracie hesitated a moment and then returned to the truck where Lauren was waiting. "I'm fine," she said. "How are things going with you and Sebastian?" Her tone was unusually cold when she said it.

That wasn't the question she was expecting. Aside from Amy, she hadn't spoken to anyone about Sebastian. Or Sutton, either. "How did you know about Sebastian and me?"

Her jaw flexed with what looked like suppressed irritation. Or anger, even. "I saw you two out at the Courtyard Shops the other day. You looked pretty cozy together."

Lauren couldn't help but notice that Gracie almost seemed jealous. Her dark brown gaze nearly cut right through her. She'd never heard of any talk about Gracie and Sebastian, but perhaps the other woman carried a torch for him from her time working for the Wingates.

"That wasn't Sebastian," she said, ignoring the shocked expression on Amy's face as her head hung out from the truck window. "That was Sutton."

Gracie flinched, her nose wrinkling in confusion. "He was driving his black BMW," she argued. "That's Sebastian's car."

"Sutton borrowed it, I guess. Maybe his car was in the shop, because he picked me up for dinner last night in his white Audi."

That was enough. A weight seemed to lift from Gracie's shoulders. "Oh. I didn't realize you were seeing Sutton. When I saw you together and Sebastian's car was there, I just assumed."

"It's a relatively new development. But nothing is going to come of it," Lauren insisted. "Things didn't go so well last night."

Regular Gracie returned fully with a sympathetic tilt of her head. "I'm sorry to hear that. Sutton is a nice guy."

"Thanks. But what about you?" Lauren asked the question lingering on her mind before fully thinking it through.

"What *about* me?"

Good question. She couldn't very well say that Gracie seemed super jealous and she wanted to know what was going on with her and Sebastian. So while she wanted to ask, she wouldn't. "I, uh, haven't seen you much lately. You usually eat at the truck once or twice a week."

"Oh," Gracie said, her expression brightening. "I'm okay, it's nothing. My stomach just hasn't been great lately, so I've been sticking to chicken noodle soup and crackers. I think it's just the stress of everything. I'll be back, I promise."

"I'm sorry you haven't felt well. But whenever you're ready, it's on the house."

Gracie smirked and crossed her arms over her chest. "Seriously? No. I didn't become a multimillionaire to shaft my friends. I'll be back, and I'll pay in full," she insisted. "I'll talk to you two later."

Lauren waved as the other woman continued down the street. That was a weird conversation. One that made her glad she hadn't actually been with Sebastian that day at the Courtyard Shops. She certainly didn't want to upset one of her friends and best customers.

"I'd really like to wrap all this up and get home at a decent time!" Amy shouted from the truck.

"Yeah, yeah," Lauren said as she stepped back into the truck to finish breaking down for the night.

She hadn't even shut the door when Amy spoke up. "So, I'm going to need more information about everything I heard just now."

Lauren sighed. Her best friend had lured her back under false pretenses. She didn't care when they got home, she just wanted information. "As long as we can talk and clean, then fine." They both returned to their tasks and Lauren relayed the prior night's revelations as succinctly as she could.

"So you're saying that was Sutton, not Sebastian, that came by the truck that day?"

"Apparently."

"And which one did you sleep with at the masquerade ball?"

"Sutton." There was no question of that. Last night as she'd lain in bed thinking about the crazy situation, the pieces finally seemed to fall into place. Things with Sebastian had never made sense, but they'd suddenly changed that day when Sutton showed up in his place. That was when the potent chemistry that had been missing had returned with a vengeance. Things between them had been amazingly good since Sutton had stepped into his brother's shoes.

At least until last night, when she'd learned it was all a lie.

"And which one is this at the window right now?"

Lauren spun around to look out the service window, where one of the Wingate twins was standing there with a bouquet in his hands looking ashamed. "Oh come on," she lamented.

"So is that Sutton or Sebastian?"

Lauren felt the familiar butterflies in her stomach. The messy hair, the crooked smile. It was Sutton for sure. But why was he here at her truck after last night? Didn't she make it perfectly clear that she needed some space?

With a groan, she walked back to the door and stepped into the street. "We're closed for the night," she said as she rounded the truck and he came into view.

He turned to her and she got a better look at the bouquet in his arms. It wasn't a bouquet of flowers. It was a bundle of fresh herbs, like rosemary, thyme, parsley and basil. The perfect offering for a chef.

"I'm not here to order food," Sutton told her. "I'm here to apologize."

Lauren wasn't sure what to do. He'd obviously put a lot of thought into a gift as he came to see her. And the way his eyes pleaded with her made her knees—and her resolve—start to soften beneath her. She'd never reacted to any man the way she reacted to Sutton. She wished she could turn it off, but despite it all, she still wanted him with a fiery passion she couldn't deny. She supposed she could at least hear what he had to say.

He held out the bouquet and she accepted it. "Thank you," she said before inhaling all the different aromatics.

"It's not enough. Not nearly enough. But it's a start. I know I have a lot of explaining to do, but I really hope you'll hear me out. I've spent the last twenty-four hours trying to figure out how to tell you how I really feel about you. If you'd just give me the chance."

A thud sounded over Lauren's shoulder and when she looked to see what made the sound, she saw her purse lying on the curb behind her. Amy waved at her through the window and the next thing she knew, the food truck engine roared to life. Amy left, leaving her with no choice but to listen to him or walk home.

Sutton gestured over to a nearby park bench. She grabbed her purse and followed him over there. Sitting side by side, she focused her eyes across the street at the line of closed shops. If she looked at him, she would give in too easily. She needed to be firm. Stand up for herself.

"Go ahead. I'm listening."

"Being a Wingate is a complicated thing," he began. "I'm not using it as an excuse, I'm just trying to explain what it's like. When we were rich and successful, it was hard to trust people because someone always wanted something from you. Whether it was someone looking for an investor, or a handout or a Sugar Daddy, it was hard to tell who was really your friend and who wasn't." He cleared his throat. "So when everything fell apart with the business, there was a new layer of suspicion added. Who was behind it all and why would they do something to us like that? It had to be someone we knew. Someone we trusted. It was a hard pill for all of us to swallow.

"That night at the masquerade party, I was not having a good time. I could feel everyone's eyes on me, judging my whole family for things we didn't do. And then I saw you and everything changed." He stopped speaking for a moment.

Lauren couldn't stop from turning to him then. He was looking at her with a pleading gaze. Desperate for her to listen and understand. Fighting the urge to reach out and touch her before she was ready.

"You didn't look at me like that," Sutton continued. "You had no idea who I was. You weren't after a lifetime of alimony payments or someone to front cash for your latest sure thing. You just wanted to dance with me. To kiss me. To give yourself to me. And that felt amazing. I couldn't wait to find out who you really were. And then you disappeared on me, leaving nothing but a mask to prove you were even real."

Lauren's gaze dropped into her lap. She felt guilty for leaving now, even though at the time it seemed like the best thing to do. The real Lauren just wasn't that exciting. Or glamorous. Or so she thought. Was it possible that he was more than interested in her, without the mask and gown?

"I thought I might never figure out who you were," Sutton explained with a sad shake of his head. "And then my brother told me that the woman he'd had a fling with at the party had showed up on his doorstep. I was so incredibly jealous. But he kept insisting it didn't feel right. So we started to wonder if there was more to it. Had we both been seduced by a woman or a pair of women set on getting information from us? Was it related somehow to the company's troubles? We had no way of knowing. So he suggested I go out with you once and see what I thought.

"The minute I laid eyes on you, I knew the problem was that you were my mystery woman, not his.

And when I touched you, it was all over for me. I was so excited to have found you, Lauren. Until you called me by my brother's name and I realized I had a big problem. I wanted to tell you the truth, but I didn't know how. So I kept my distance. I didn't want to let things go too far while you thought I was Sebastian."

She closed her eyes as she realized the truth of why he hadn't kissed her again since that first night. "I thought maybe you didn't want me. That without the excitement of the mask and my makeover, you just weren't that into it. I've felt like an obligation since the beginning, especially with Sebastian."

Sutton reached out to cup her cheek and turn her gaze to meet his. "That couldn't be farther from the truth, Lauren. I've wanted nothing more than to hold you. And kiss you and make love to you again. But when I did it, I wanted you to call out my name, not my brother's."

She gasped at his words. They were sincerer, more intense than she ever could've imagined. A man had never spoken to her that way before.

Lauren couldn't resist leaning into him. He met her advance with his mouth, pressing his lips firmly against hers. It was just like she remembered from the club. Passionate. Hungry. He groaned as her tongue slid along his and invited more.

His arms wrapped around her waist, tugging her closer to him on the bench. Lauren ached for the feel of his fingertips pressed into her flesh and the hard wall of his chest beneath her own. She wanted to unbutton his collar and touch him like she had before. But not here, on a city park bench. If she'd learned nothing else from her conversation with Gracie today, it was that people were always watching. She wanted to take him home and do whatever she wanted without witnesses or a hard pool table limiting her.

Lauren pulled away from his lips, near breathless. "I know your name now," she said with a wicked smile.

Eight

As they drove back to Sutton's house, Lauren wasn't entirely sure this was a good idea. He had apologized for deceiving her, and she had accepted his apology, so they were okay there, at least. But she wondered if it was too soon to sleep with him again. She was just coming to terms with him being who he really was.

But in that moment, when Sutton looked at her with desire blazing in his eyes, she didn't care about whether or not it was the wrong thing to do right now. None of those reasons mattered anymore. She had spent every night since the masquerade ball lying in bed, thinking about being with her big, bad wolf again. When she met Sebastian and her expectations crumbled, she thought she might never have that chance again.

And now here she was, standing in Sutton's luxuriously appointed bedroom, slipping out of her chef's jacket. And it was about to happen. She couldn't deny herself what she'd fantasized about any longer when it was here for the taking.

His green eyes never left hers as he shrugged out of his own coat. He was trying to focus on what he was doing, but she could tell it was difficult for him, with her slowly pulling her shirt up over her head and exposing the red-and-white floral bra she was wearing underneath. She tossed the top over a chair with her coat. Then she reached down to unbutton her jeans.

It was at that point that Sutton froze in place, no longer able to undress himself while watching her at the same time. She supposed this time was different for them both. They not only knew each other's names, but the lights were on. They could see everything the other had to offer. All of the things they'd felt, but not seen, were on display.

Despite how much she wanted to quickly slip out of her clothes and press up against him, she was going to take her time. She turned her back to Sutton, giving him a full view of her rear end as the denim peeled away and exposed the red cotton bikini-cut panties she wore beneath them.

She hadn't had seduction on her mind when she dressed this morning, but he didn't seem to mind. Sutton groaned aloud as she bent over and stepped out of the pants. And when she turned back around to face him wearing nothing but her bra and panties, he was standing exactly as she'd left him.

Walking over to him, she pushed his shirt off his shoulders until it slipped to the floor. She let her hands run over his bare chest and arms, something she hadn't been able to do before, and enjoyed the firm muscles that twitched beneath the silk of his skin. He seemed to almost be holding his breath the entire time she touched him, yet still cooperating with her exploration until Lauren reached for the button of his trousers. Then his hand came to hers, covering her fingers and keeping her from going any further.

"Not so fast," Sutton growled. "We're not in a rush tonight."

Lauren pouted for a moment but had to admit that she was looking forward to a long, leisurely night of lovemaking in a real bed with all of their clothes off. The quick, passionate tryst they'd had at the club was the kind that sacrificed comfort for a driving need, but tonight, they could do anything and everything they wanted without interruption or discomfort.

"Wait for me in the bed and I'll be right back,"

he said, giving her a playful slap on the behind as he walked away.

Lauren sauntered slowly to the bed, knowing he was watching her. She slipped off her bra and panties, fully nude at last, and then pushed aside the steel-gray comforter before she crawled onto the soft, welcoming bed.

When she was settled in, he tossed aside the last of his own clothing and disappeared into his bathroom. He returned a moment later with a handful of foil packets in his hand. Her eyes widened as she tried to count how many, but gave up when he tossed them into a pile on the nightstand.

Lauren crawled to the edge of the bed and perched on her knees as he stood beside it. She ran her hands over him again, toying with his chest hair and following the line of it down his stomach with her fingertips. At that point, her cheeks flushed. His desire for her was fully on display in the well-lit room. Her palms tingled with the need to stroke him, but he was just out of her reach. She knew she would get in trouble again if she pushed it.

As if he sensed her devious thoughts, he took a step back. Sutton flipped on the lamp on the dresser, killing the overhead fixture. The harsh glare disappeared, casting them in a dim, romantic glow. He returned to her then, pressing forward until she tumbled backward on the mattress and he was covering her body with his.

The heat and the weight of him against her bare skin was soothing. When he dipped his head to kiss her, the fall nip in the air seemed to disappear. His touch heated the very blood in her veins, the spreading warmth amplifying with every pound of her heart in her chest. She relished the slide of his tongue along hers. His every caress was expertly targeted to her most sensitive parts as though he'd managed to memorize her body in that single night together.

When his thumb brushed over the hard peak of her nipple, Lauren gasped. Then he sucked it into the scorching heat of his mouth and her back arched sharply off the bed. He was relentless in his pleasurable assault, teasing her with his teeth and tongue even as his hands glided down her hip and dipped between her thighs.

"Sutton!" she cried as he made explosive contact with her feminine center.

He lifted his head and looked down at her. "Say it again," he demanded with his hand still slowly circling over her flesh.

"Sutton," she repeated with a desperate edge in her voice.

"I love the sound of my name on your lips. I'm going to make you scream it all night, if I have any say about it."

He smothered her response when he kissed her again. His tongue echoed the movements of his hand, slowly sliding in and out of her mouth. She squirmed beneath him, panting as he drew her ever closer to the edge of her release, again and again, always backing away before she shattered.

Then Sutton reached for the condoms he'd left on the nightstand. He sat back on his knees to roll the latex sheath over himself, then slipped back between her thighs. His mouth found hers again and with a subtle shift of his weight, he was pressing against her entrance. But there he stopped.

A whimper of disappointment caught in her throat. Lauren couldn't wait any longer for him. She cradled Sutton's hips between her thighs. Impatiently, she gripped his hips and drew him forward. He moved with her and, before she knew it, she got what she wanted. Every thick inch of Sutton was buried deep inside of her. The moment was everything she'd remembered it to be and more with the visual of him hovering over her.

Sutton eased back and thrust into her a second time with a sharp hiss. Lauren lifted her hips, taking in all that she could. Her body strained and flexed around him, her muscles tightening their grip until he groaned into her throat.

Leaning down, he kissed her and started moving at a quicker pace. Eventually, Lauren had to tear her lips from his so she could cry out with each pleasurable drive into her.

They fell into an easy rhythm, her hips rising

off the bed to meet his every advance. The pleasure easily built up inside her again, this time with more intensity than before. She clawed futilely with her nails at the blankets beneath her. Trying with all her might to find something to hold on to, something to keep her anchored when her orgasm hit like a tidal wave.

And she was almost there. She closed her eyes as her whole body tensed and her whimpers increased in intensity.

"Yes," Sutton coaxed, seeming to recognize the familiar sounds of her impending release. "That's it. Don't hold back, Lauren. I want to watch you come apart this time."

He increased his pace and it pushed her over the edge. The waves of pleasure crashed in on her all at once, wracking her body with the pulsating sensations. She gasped and cried his name, writhing beneath him. And when it was all over, she opened her eyes and found that he'd watched every moment of her undoing.

"You're beautiful," he said, looking down at her.

She didn't feel beautiful. Especially not at the moment. She'd come here straight from a long day at the food truck without a stitch of makeup on and her hair in its usual bun. Her orgasm had no doubt left her flushed and sweaty, her lips were swollen from his kisses and her cheeks felt a little raw from the rough stubble of his jaw on her delicate skin.

She wrinkled her nose, smirking dismissively at his observation.

"No," he argued, dipping down to kiss her forcefully and erase the disagreement from her lips. "It's true. You're beautiful. And talented. And amazing in every way I can think of. And since it's my opinion, I'm not arguing with you about any of it."

At that, Lauren laughed and pushed some stray hair out of her face. "You've spent your whole life surrounded by rich debutantes who spend all their time in expensive salons and day spas to stay flawless. Some of those women I saw at the club looked like movie stars up close."

"And?"

Her eyes widened and she swallowed hard. How could it be possible that she ranked up there with women like that? It was a nice sentiment, but too hard for her to believe.

"And… I don't know that I'm in their league."

"You're not. You're in a league of your own."

Lauren could only shake her head.

With a growl of irritation, he flipped over, rolling onto his back with Lauren sitting astride him. She squealed with the sudden reversal, their bodies never disconnecting. "Making love to you with the lights on is incredible. And since I'm inside *you*, hard as a rock, and not with any of those other women, I think I'm the best judge of what I like."

His hands gripped her hips and he started thrusting into her from underneath. Lauren braced her hands on his chest and moved with him. His eyes never left her face and, in seconds, his jaw was tight and his fingertips were pressing insistently into the flesh of her hips.

It occurred to her then that if he really liked to watch her, she might know just how to push him over the edge. Lauren arched her back, loosening her hair from its tight bun and shaking it out until the brown waves fell to her shoulders. Then she ran her fingers through it, thrusting her breasts out as she rocked her hips against him.

He reached out to cover her breasts with his hands and she put her own palms over his. Holding tight, she moved faster, pressing against him for leverage.

"I'm never turning the lights out again..." he said in a whispered groan, his words interrupted by the powerful rush of his release. She rode out the storm, finally collapsing onto the mattress beside him in a state of physical, mental and emotional exhaustion.

This. This was exactly what she'd been craving since their first night together. Not just the pleasure, but the closeness, the intimacy of being in Sutton's arms. To have him touch her and know exactly what she liked. To hold him close and feel like someone out in the world cared about her. Wanted her. Needed her. It was as though the final puzzle piece of their romance had clicked into place. It was an amazing feeling, and yet, a scary one. Lauren could feel her resistance fading. If she wasn't careful, she might start to have feelings for him.

If she didn't already.

Sutton scooped her into his arms and pulled her back against the hard wall of his chest. "Beautiful," he whispered, planting a kiss on her bare shoulder as they both drifted off to sleep.

"I see you two have made up."

Sutton and Lauren were sitting at the kitchen island together enjoying their first cup of coffee while her clothes were being washed. After last night, with only a few hours' sleep, he needed a little perk of caffeine to get through the day. Or he would if he had something to do. He'd happily be in bed asleep if not for Lauren having to get up and go to her trucks.

When he turned his head, he saw his brother Sebastian standing at the bottom of the stairs looking at them. "Good morning to you, dear brother. And yes, we did make up. We made up all night as a matter of fact."

Sebastian rolled his eyes at Sutton's oversharing. "Well, good for you, I guess." He went to the coffeepot to pour his own cup. As he did, his brother's gaze drifted briefly over to where Lauren was sitting in nothing but one of Sutton's oversize T-shirts.

"Her clothes are in the dryer," Sutton explained.

Sebastian shook his head. “I have no problem with half-naked women in my kitchen. I just prefer when they’re mine.”

“It’s fun living with you, too.” He raised his mug to toast to his uptight twin.

Lauren turned toward Sebastian and studied him for a moment before looking back at Sutton. “Did you say that you two are identical twins?”

“Yep,” Sutton confirmed. “Genetically identical, socially opposite.”

“Interesting. Well, now that I have both of you in the same room, I don’t know how I ever confused the two of you.”

“I know, I’m so much more attractive than Sebastian,” Sutton teased.

“It’s not that. You do physically look alike, you just carry yourselves differently. It’s a whole different vibe. Of course, it helped your cause that I didn’t know Sebastian had a twin to begin with. It just seemed like he had a laid-back alter ego or something. You couldn’t fool me now the way you did before.”

“Is that a challenge?” Sutton teased.

“Don’t you dare,” Lauren warned with a pointed finger. “I’ve had enough of those games.”

“Don’t worry, Lauren,” Sebastian said. “Sutton doesn’t like pretending to be me. He has to comb his hair and wear decent clothes.”

"And drive boring cars and talk about boring things," his twin quipped.

Sebastian sighed. "Do you have any brothers or sisters, Lauren?"

"No. It's just me."

"Ahh. Then you will never truly know the depths of what I have to deal with being the oldest of five. Three of them aren't much trouble, but this one..." Sebastian gestured his thumb at Sutton when he got up to get more cream from the refrigerator. "Trouble from the womb."

Sutton turned back to the two of them. "I'm a delight. Everyone thinks so, just ask around town. And it's not like I'm a lost cause crashing on people's couches and borrowing money. I did a damn good job as the CFO of the family business. Things were booming with the two of us at the helm. And not because we were smuggling drugs in our planes."

Sebastian groaned. "Can we talk about something else, please? *Anything* else."

Lauren smiled and took advantage of his offer. "Okay. Here's a new topic. Sebastian, now that we've determined that I was Sutton's mystery woman, what are you going to do about finding yours?"

That was a good question. Sutton was curious to hear the answer himself. His brother wasn't really the kind to have a fling at a party. The mere fact that he had meant that the lady had a magnetic hold on Sebastian. Sutton never thought he would see the day that his super analytical twin would be entranced by a female to the point of abandoning his usual good sense.

But would he do anything about it? Sutton was more prone to be the hunter than his brother. Sebastian was always too busy for things like that.

His twin set down his coffee mug and gazed thoughtfully into the living room. "I don't know what I'm going to do. I guess I never expected to hear from her again. When you showed up at the house, I was excited by the idea of having a second chance with her, but now that I'm back at square one, I'm not sure where to start."

"I've got a list of party guests that Beth gave me," Sutton offered. "I asked her for it when I was hunting for my masked beauty." He leaned in and pressed a kiss against Lauren's neck. He liked that her hair was always up in a bun. It gave him free access to the long, bare line of her throat and he could plant kisses beneath her ear whenever he felt like it. "Since I've found her, you can have it."

He enjoyed watching the blush rise to her cheeks. Her every thought and feeling was etched on her face, which made having sex with her even by dim lamplight particularly exciting. Their first time together had been in total darkness, never mind the masks. Now he could see every thrill, every pulsating ripple of pleasure dance across her face.

"I may take you up on that. But for now, I'm heading out for a while."

"Where to?" It was awfully early for his equally unemployed brother to be up, dressed and ready to go out the door.

"To the club. I'm going to meet a few people there." Sebastian finished off his coffee and put the mug in the sink. "I'll be back this afternoon."

Sutton gently stroked Lauren's back through his T-shirt as he watched his brother go. "He's really into her, whomever she is."

Lauren turned to him with a wrinkled nose. "How can you tell?"

"Because he's considering looking for her. That's huge for him. The family and the business have always come before his social life."

"Well, maybe since his calendar is cleared, he has time to look for his missing lover."

"Maybe so. Honestly, I feel like I'm going mad with all this time on my hands." He leaned in to nibble on her neck again. "I wish you didn't work so much so you could help me occupy the time."

Lauren giggled and squirmed away. "Well, not everyone was the CFO of a Fortune 500 company. Some of us are the CEO, CFO, payroll manager, line cook and head bottle washer of a Fortune 100,000 company. I've got to bust my ass every day to keep my head above water and build my business."

Sutton lowered himself down onto the stool beside her. “You know, I could help you out.”

“What? Can you cook?”

“No, not like that,” he laughed. “I managed the finances of our whole company. The marketing department reported to me, as well. I have a great head for management. Let me use it to help you out.”

Lauren’s face said it all—she didn’t know how to politely tell him no. That meant she wouldn’t. “I don’t know, Sutton. The restaurant business isn’t like your company.”

“Obviously, there are differences. But I know how to get good word of mouth going. I’m great with promotion. I can help you brainstorm ideas. Really. Like, tell me your ultimate goal for the business.”

“What?”

Sutton turned Lauren to face him on the stool and gripped her shoulders gently. She was being stubborn. He wasn’t sure if she was just used to being a one woman show, or if she didn’t trust his ideas. His own confidence waivered slightly at her resistance. He wouldn’t blame her for rejecting his help. Who wanted advice from someone who’d been ousted by the board of directors, after all? He tamped down his own doubts. “Just do me a favor and close your eyes.”

She eventually complied, but not without the line of concern returning between her brows. “Okay. Now what?”

"Picture yourself ten years from now. You're at the pinnacle of your career. You have everything you've ever wanted to achieve and more. Visualize it in your mind, make it real with all your senses. Then tell me what you see."

Lauren took a deep breath before she answered. "I have my own successful restaurant here in Royal. One without wheels."

"That's great." He wouldn't say it aloud, but a chef of Lauren's caliber didn't need to be cooking in a truck. She needed a real, brick-and-mortar restaurant where she could take her culinary creations to the next level. "What else do you see?"

"White walls, colorful paintings. There are people at every table, happy…eating…talking. It's beautiful. And it smells amazing."

"Have you sold the food trucks?" he asked.

She thought for a moment. "I don't know. Maybe I have staff to run them for me while I focus on the restaurant."

"Do you have one restaurant or a chain? Remember, this is your ultimate dream. You can have anything."

Lauren opened her eyes and looked at him. "One is enough for me. I'm no Bobby Flay or Wolfgang Puck. I want more than just my name on the sign, I want to be the executive chef in the kitchen. A chain is…too much. I just want to have my restaurant and to make people happy with my cooking. Isn't that enough?"

Sutton realized he'd overstepped and tried to backpedal with a bright smile. "Of course, it's enough. Whatever you want. I just want to make sure you're letting yourself dream big enough. Your food is amazing. You could have a chain of restaurants if you wanted to, someday. Or one amazing place, if you'd prefer. I think you could put that Italian place in Dallas to shame. Hey—maybe you could do a pop-up event like they did and get a taste for the permanent restaurant life."

Lauren shook her head. "While I'd love to, that place was successful enough to be able to do things I could never do, because I don't have the money. You have to have money to make money in a business like this. With most restaurants folding within five years, I'm lucky to still be open, much less thriving."

"I don't think it would take that much to pull it together. You don't have to make it as fancy as they were. You could scale back the decor. Maybe work with some local businesses to rent dishware or get floral arrangements in exchange for free advertising. I know a lot of people in this town. I bet I could pull a few strings to make it happen."

Lauren looked at him with eyes that wanted to believe it was possible. But she wasn't certain of herself. Or of him. He could tell.

"Next Saturday," Sutton declared. "Lauren Roberts's Eatery is coming to Royal, Texas."

Nine

Lauren walked around the big, empty space that would be her restaurant dining room come Saturday night. It was the empty spot on the square she'd always eyed for her future location. It had been a restaurant a while back, so it had a fully outfitted kitchen and the layout she needed up front. Honestly, she never expected to get this location for the pop-up, but true to his word, Sutton had contacts. He knew who owned this building and contacted him about letting her use it for free under the premise that if it was a success, she might rent it from him permanently. Since it was sitting empty and earning no revenue, the owner had agreed.

He'd also apparently called in every favor he had to make this work. The local florist was providing her with the florist's choice of twenty, small, table-top arrangements and a larger one for the hostess desk. The party rental company in town was bringing her tables, chairs, linens, dishes, flatware and glasses in exchange for a full-page ad on the back of her menu. The local paper had even interviewed her for an article about the pop-up event, which had driven curious readers to her Instagram account, nearly tripling her followers and even her sales at the truck that week.

Sutton had taken care of everything. He had gone over and above to make her successful. It was costing her almost nothing aside from some temporary labor up front to make it happen. It was… incredibly intimidating.

She was grateful, but also apprehensive about the whole thing. What if she didn't succeed? He was pushing so hard to make her into this great restauranteur. He'd provided her with every tool she could possibly need because he believed she had the talent. But a lot of people had talent and still failed. What if even his best efforts couldn't turn her into a culinary star?

Lauren took a deep breath and tried to push away her doubts. All she could do was her best. She needed to make the most of the unexpected gift she'd been given, and let the chips fall where they may.

Now that she was inside the building, she could see the space would need a lot of TLC if it were ever to be her dream restaurant. The walls could use patching, and some new paint and crown molding. The dark green carpet needed replacement and the florescent overhead lighting was too harsh for a romantic or chic dining space. But it would work. She had to keep reminding herself that updating this space was a problem she would love to have and one that was dependent on the success of this pop-up event.

Today wasn't about the end product she envisioned in her mind with Sutton. It was about putting together a place good enough for one night in the hopes that one day, it could be more. Planting her hands on her hips with a newly determined air, she knew she could turn this dream into a reality.

She went back into the kitchen and was amazed by how much space she would have to cook here. There could easily be seven or eight people back here prepping dishes—a proper kitchen staff for a busy restaurant of this size—and there would be plenty of room to work. Considering that she and Amy were constantly bumping into one another in the truck, it was a welcome change. Food trucks weren't particularly spacious.

Or prestigious.

Lauren sighed and leaned against the stainless-steel countertop. Her can-do attitude deflated a little as she crossed her arms protectively over her chest. She wasn't quite as excited about all of this as she thought she would be. It was a chance she didn't think she'd have for years, easily. But if she thought hard enough about what was dragging down her thoughts, she knew it wasn't just her fear of failure. It was what her failure might mean for her future with Sutton.

In the last few days, as he'd spent all his free time trying to pull this event together, Lauren had realized the full extent of the Wingate's influence in Royal. She knew his family was rich. They were club members, after all. But she was slowly beginning to realize that they were damn near royalty here in town. Even with scandal looming over their heads.

Maybe she just didn't run in the right circles to realize it sooner. Royal had a lot of rich and influential people, so one was just the same as another to her. She didn't fit in amongst them and only interacted long enough to sell them the occasional lunch, so it never mattered if she kept up with the hierarchy of Royal society.

That was probably at the root of her worries today. She didn't fit in, yet through a twist of fate, she was dating one of Royal's most eligible princes. Even having feelings for him. She was just a commoner, and she was okay with her station in town, but she was beginning to wonder if Sutton was okay with it, as well.

Under the guise of helping, he really seemed to be pushing her to do more, faster than she planned. Do a pop-up event, open a "real" restaurant, sell the food trucks… It was the path she hoped to take someday, but his insistence made Lauren feel like maybe she wasn't good enough for Sutton as she was. They'd been out in public together, so he wasn't hiding her away in embarrassment, but they hadn't spoken to anyone else when they were out, either. If he had to introduce her to people he knew, would he tell them she was a chef and conveniently leave out the trucks? Was a restaurant with wheels not esteemed enough for the Wingates and their club-going cronies?

Lauren looked down at her fingernails, which she'd been nervously chewing the last few days. Her makeover manicure was basically destroyed now, with chipped paint and rough edges. And she'd noticed this morning when she looked in the mirror that her highlights had grown out, showing dark roots that needed a touch-up. She probably needed a blowout, too, to smooth her naturally unruly waves. She hadn't been wearing makeup or dressing up much unless they were going someplace nice.

She looked like the Lauren she recognized again.

But somehow she didn't feel like that was good enough anymore.

All in all, she just didn't feel like Cinderella ready for the ball any longer. The beautiful and mysterious woman that had enchanted the prince from behind a mask was gone. Now Sutton was left with the real Lauren and, although he'd never said anything to make her think he was disappointed with reality, he seemed determined to mold her and her life into something more presentable, like Pygmalion or Henry Higgins. An unpolished food truck chef was just not the kind of girl a Wingate wanted to take home to mother.

And yet... Lauren brushed a stray strand of hair from her face. He was helping her achieve her dream. Perhaps she needed to look at it that way and push her doubts aside. She didn't want to be a food truck owner forever, either. It had always been a stepping-stone for her on the way to her dream restaurant. And while Sutton might have grand ideas about a chain of Eateries across the country, she would be happy with this one and the help he gave her to get there.

"Enough moping," she said aloud to the empty kitchen. Regardless of *why* he'd helped her, she was truly grateful, and tomorrow The Eatery would be a reality, if for just a single day. That meant that today, she had a lot of work to do. She'd closed down the trucks for a few days so she could have her staff focused on helping her, and she'd need every man on deck to make it happen. Amy, Javier and his assistant Ed from truck two, plus a few wait-staff temps she'd hired from a local agency would be meeting her here at ten.

Today, they needed to focus on cleaning the space up and getting it ready. Then she had to plan the menu, go shopping for necessary ingredients and establish a game plan for tomorrow night. It was almost overwhelming, but she kept telling herself she could do this. She made multiple dishes every day in a truck. She could handle dinner service with a team of helpers.

A chime at the front door drew her attention from the kitchen. "We're here!" she heard Amy shout from up front.

Lauren went to the front of the house to greet her truck staff. The three of them stood there with dubious expressions on their faces as they looked around. Since she had already gotten that out of the way, she was prepared to be the enthusiastic leader they needed to make this happen.

"It doesn't look like much, but it has a ton of potential," she started. "It hasn't been used in a while, so we need to start with a good, thorough cleaning. Ed and Javier, why don't you start with the kitchen. I've got a box of cleaning supplies back there already. Amy, help me get the front of the house ready. The rental company is coming with chairs and tables for us to set up in about two hours."

Everyone set out to do their jobs without question and within a few hours, things really started to take shape. Tables and chairs were delivered and went into their places, and, by lights out, the kitchen was stocked with food, supplies and all the dishes they could possibly need.

"I'll pick up the menus at the printshop in the morning," Amy said as she slipped her laptop into her bag. Ed and Javier had already left for the night, hauling out bags of trash and cleaning supplies with them.

"Thank you for all your help," Lauren said.

"Of course," Amy said. "No one wants this event to be successful more than I do."

"And why is that?" Lauren asked, expecting her best friend to say something about seeing her achieve her dream.

Amy smiled and held open the door for the two of them to step out into the parking lot. "So we can work in a building where I don't have to walk to a gas station down the road every time I have to use the bathroom."

Lauren chuckled as she locked up the door and walked over to her car. That was more like the Amy she knew. "Think good thoughts for tomorrow," she said. "We need this to be a success."

"It will be," Amy said. "I have no doubt of it."

She watched her friend get into her car and then did the same. As she pulled out of the lot and headed home, she hoped Amy was right. Because if it wasn't a success and she was right about Sutton's real motivations, the end of The Eatery would be the end of their relationship, too.

Sutton was blown away by how busy The Eatery was tonight. When he pulled up, the parking lot was full and he had to walk a whole block back to the restaurant. Inside, there was a crowd waiting by the door and people at every table. With only an hour left in the service, he couldn't imagine how much work it would take to feed the remaining customers and wrap things up for the night.

Folks seemed happy to wait, though, and he could guess as to why. Not only was the space filled with the most mouthwatering scents he'd ever smelled, but the room had been completely transformed since the last time he saw it.

It was nothing permanent—it still had the same paint, overhead lighting and carpeting—but everything she could change, she did. For starters, they'd kept the lights off, choosing to light the space with tabletop flameless candles, strands of Edison bulbs overhead and tall lamps in the corners. That hid a multitude of sins. Instead of white linens, each table had either a red, yellow, blue or dark green tablecloth. It might have been all the rental place had available for free on a Saturday night, but Lauren made it work by pairing it with brightly colored posters on the walls and bright yellow-and-red flower arrangements.

If this was what Lauren could do with some donations and a couple of days, he couldn't wait to see what the real restaurant would be like. He wished he could help it become a reality and perhaps someday he could, but this was a great start and he was proud to have a part in it.

Sutton had done everything he could think of, called in every favor he had to make it happen, and he was thrilled by the result. And honestly, he was thrilled to have something to do with his time. The last few days, he had finally felt like he had some direction again. He'd been drifting without his job at the family business to anchor him. If Lauren hadn't dropped into his life as both a pleasurable distraction and a fun project to occupy his mind, he was sure he would've gone mad by now.

Looking around, Sutton beamed with a sense of pride he hadn't felt in ages. No, this was more than just something to keep him busy. *She* was more than just something to keep him busy. He was helping an amazing woman achieve amazing things. She just needed a little help, a little push. And she was making the most of it.

A few people waiting for a table glanced at Sutton and murmured to one another. It was a common occurrence lately, and he had tried not to let it bother him. But now, the thought crossed his mind that maybe the best thing he could do for Lauren was leave. Sutton had given her a boost, but perhaps taking a step back now would be for the best. He wouldn't want his family's tainted reputation to spoil this for her after she'd worked so hard.

Perhaps he could say hello, so she wouldn't think he blew off her big night, then he would leave.

"Sir, my wait list is full for the night, so we're not taking any more names."

Sutton turned to the young woman who'd been hired as hostess for the night. From the weary expression on her face, he wasn't the first one she'd had to turn away this evening. "That's okay, I'm not staying. I'm just going to go in back and give the chef a kiss, if you don't mind."

The woman's eyes widened for a minute, and then she smiled. "Oh, you must be Mr. Wingate. Chef Roberts said you could go on back to the kitchen whenever you arrived. She also said to get you a table no matter how busy, so just give me a moment and I'll see what I can do."

"There's no need," he said. "Let the others have it." He would much rather leave a table for someone who hadn't yet discovered the brilliance of Lauren's cooking. He was already a huge fan of hers in more ways than one.

"You're sure? Her beef Wellington has been earning rave reviews tonight."

"I'm sure it has, but I'll have the chance to try it another time. Thank you." He made his way through a maze of tables to the swinging door that separated the dining room from the kitchen. Before he could reach it, it swung open and Lauren herself stepped out with a plate in each hand.

"Sutton!" she said in surprise.

She looked excited and exhausted all at once, but she grinned when she saw him. A strand of chestnut hair had escaped her bun, so he reached out and tucked it behind her ear. He'd only intended to lean in and give her a quick kiss on the cheek, but he found himself cupping her face in his hands and planting a firm, warm kiss on the lips that promised more to come later.

Lauren seemed dazed and flushed for a moment as she clutched the plates in her hands. "I'm glad to see you, too," she replied with a sassy grin curling her lips.

He looked at the dishes she held out. "Are you the executive chef or the waitress tonight? If you need waitstaff, I can roll up my sleeves and jump in."

"No, we're fine. This is a special delivery for a special patron," Lauren said and gestured over to the table where Gracie Diaz was sitting with a friend. "Come with me."

Sutton followed her over to where Lauren personally delivered the meals to Gracie and her friend. "Ladies, I have special plates just for this table, as Gracie is one of my first and most outspoken supporters. Bon appétit."

Gracie lit up at the sight of Lauren and the food in front of her. "This looks amazing. It's *all* amazing." She got up from her seat and wrapped Lauren in a hug. "I don't even need to taste it to know that you absolutely have to open a restaurant, girl. I need more than just a quick lunch on the go. I need your haute cuisine, too."

Lauren smiled and rested a hand on Gracie's shoulder. "Tonight has been a great success, thanks to everyone's help, especially Sutton's, but I think a permanent location is still a ways off for me."

Gracie studied Lauren for a moment and shook her head. "No."

"No?" Lauren looked confused by her refusal.

"No, I don't want to wait. What if I offered to invest in your restaurant? As a silent partner, of course. You don't need any input from me. But I could give you what you need to get started."

Both Sutton and Lauren shot to attention when they heard Gracie's offer. He was delighted for Lauren and jealous of Gracie all at once. He wished he could've been the one to bankroll Lauren's dream, but he was happy Gracie had the ability to do it when he couldn't.

"Are you serious?" Lauren's hand clutched at her

chest as though she were trying to hold her heart in her rib cage.

"Absolutely. I wouldn't joke about something like that. You're an incredible chef and I believe in your talents. So much so that I'm willing to risk my own money to make it a reality. I'd honestly been toying with the idea for a while and now that I've seen what you could do with a temporary place, I know it's the right decision. What good is all this money I won, if it's just sitting in a bank and I can't help my friends?"

"I don't know what to say." Lauren's eyes were glassy with tears.

"Say that you're happy to take my money and do something awesome with it. I'll write you a check tomorrow morning to get things started and if you need more, just ask. I know all you need is enough capital to get this place up and running. And when you're the success I know you'll be, you can pay me back and buy me out."

Lauren's jaw dropped and she lunged forward to wrap Gracie in another hug. "Thank you so much!"

When she pulled away she turned back to Sutton. He'd never seen her face so full of pure excitement before. It was like Christmas morning for her. She threw her arms around his neck and he lifted her up off the ground in a bear hug.

"We're opening a restaurant!" he shouted to everyone in the dining room and he was answered with the roar of applause filling the space.

He held Lauren close, brushing away the rogue strand of hair again. “Congratulations, Chef Roberts.”

“Can you believe it?” she said.

“I can. You deserve it. Your whole life is about to change. The whole town is going to know your name before too long.”

The expression on Lauren’s face flickered for a moment and she nodded. “Things will change,” she agreed, with a little less enthusiasm in her voice. Untangling from his arms, she turned back to Gracie. “A bottle of wine on the house!” she said.

“Oh no,” Gracie insisted. “I’m driving tonight. But I’ve heard there’s an amazing dessert on the menu tonight. I’ll gladly accept a free sweet.”

“You bet. I’ll set aside a pumpkin crème brûlée for you. We’re close to running out.”

“It sounds wonderful.”

Lauren nodded. “Enjoy your dinner, ladies,” she said before turning back to the kitchen. “Have you eaten yet, Sutton?”

“No,” he replied as he followed in her wake. “That’s okay, though. You need to focus on your future customers. I just wanted to say hello and get out of your way.”

She wrinkled her nose at him and pushed open the swinging door. “Absolutely not. You’re a customer, too. Come on back and I'll make you a plate if you're worried about taking up a table. What do you want?"

He supposed that if he hid in the kitchen, his presence couldn't cause a stir with customers. And he was hungry. "Anything." He meant it. He doubted anything she made would be bad.

Lauren smiled. "I need a Wellington on the fly please!"

"Yes, Chef!" Javier yelled from the far side of the kitchen.

"And I need a crème brûlée set aside for table 8."

"Yes, Chef!" Amy echoed, turning to the refrigerator to move the dish aside.

"I've also got some great news to share with all of you."

The chaos in the kitchen stilled for a moment, with everyone looking at the two of them standing near the entrance.

"What is it?" Amy asked.

"Guys, we've got an investor! We're opening a real restaurant!"

Everyone in the kitchen dropped what they were doing and rushed over to give Lauren a hug. There were words of encouragement and excitement, but the celebration was short-lived. After each person had their moment with Lauren, they headed back to the dishes and tasks they had in progress. Apparently there was no such thing as downtime in a kitchen during dinner service, no matter the good news.

Sutton watched as they all returned to their stations, but this time, with a new spring in their steps and smiles on their faces. Lauren stepped right back into her role, calling out meals from the tickets the servers brought back and finishing off plates with garnishes as they came up for service.

"I've got a Wellington and a chicken roulette for table four!" she shouted and slammed a bell to call the servers back to the kitchen.

In a well-choreographed dance, the servers scooped up the plates, moved around Sutton and each other, and disappeared back through the door in a moment. It was chaos of the likes he'd never seen before, but he could see the rhythm of it, too. It was nothing like the corporate environment he was used to, and he was the first to admit he wasn't sure he could hack the high pressure of the kitchen.

Then again, maybe he wasn't suited for the corporate environment either. He thought he did a good job running things with his brother after his father passed away, and yet everything had unraveled so quickly and easily. Someone hated them all enough to destroy his family, their careers and his father's legacy. If they didn't catch the culprit behind it all and there was no future for him with Wingate Enterprises, Sutton honestly wasn't sure what he was suited for.

He didn't have a passion for his work like Lauren did. He'd been groomed his whole life to run his father's company and he'd never given anything else much thought. If the person who set them all up succeeded in getting Sutton and Sebastian put behind bars, there would be a bleak future for both of them. In a year's time, Lauren would be fulfilling all her dreams, and Sutton would be… He shook his head. He didn't want to know.

"Here you go, sir. One beef Wellington with whipped potatoes and grilled asparagus." Amy approached him with a beautifully assembled plate and gestured over to the side of the kitchen where there was a clear bit of stainless-steel countertop and a stool where he could sit. "The best seat in the house," she added with a smile.

He took a seat and accepted the plate with anticipation. This was just what he needed to get those dark thoughts out of his mind. It had been years since he'd had a good beef Wellington and he was certain this would be one of the best. One bite later, he knew he was right. He didn't know where Lauren went to culinary school or what great chefs she'd studied under, but she had a gift. A gift that deserved a classy environment, not a cramped truck parked along a curb.

Sutton couldn't wait for service to end tonight.

He wanted to take Lauren home to celebrate her success. She deserved it. And hopefully when everything was said and done, he would still deserve her.

Ten

Lauren opened the front door of her house later that night and found Sutton standing on her front porch with a bottle of expensive French champagne in his hand.

"Ooh…" she said, accepting the bottle and looking over the label. "You'd think we were celebrating."

Sutton stepped inside and was quick to slip out of his suit coat and tug at his tie. "I know you're probably exhausted, but we can't let this moment pass without a little bubbly."

Lauren nodded and locked the door behind him. It had been the longest day she could remember, but she was oddly energized. Her mind was buzzing with everything that had happened and she couldn't sleep even if she tried. "I'm sorry I'm underdressed for the occasion." She'd showered when she got home and was wearing only a silk robe when he came to the door.

Sutton eyed the loosely tied robe and the damp strands of her hair with a look of stark appreciation in his gaze and shook his head. "You're overdressed in my opinion."

Lauren chuckled. She had a little something in the closet he might like. "Open this up while I change."

He walked over to take the bottle back from her and carried it into the kitchen. From her bedroom, she could hear the loud pop of the cork when he succeeded. She quickly slipped on a rose-colored chemise with lacy trim along the hem and a deep V that plunged between her breasts and made her way back to where he was waiting for her. Pulling two crystal flutes down from the cabinet, she set them down on the quartz countertop and watched while he poured them each a glass.

Sutton set down the bottle and picked up the flutes filled with golden bubbly liquid. His gaze met hers and dipped lower to admire her new attire. He swallowed hard and his fingers tightened around the delicate crystal stems of the glasses. His chest swelled with a deep breath before his eyes met hers again. There was a hard glint of desire there. There was no question that he wanted her. The intensity of his stare stole the air from her lungs.

Tonight was special. They had both worked hard to make it a success and their celebration should be equally rejoiceful. With a sly smile, Lauren eyed the champagne and got an idea. Without accepting the glass he offered, she turned her back to Sutton and strolled out of the kitchen. As she crossed the threshold into her bedroom, her fingertips curled around the hem of her chemise, pulling it up and over her head. Her damp hair spilled back down around her shoulders, tickling her bare shoulder blades. She tossed the barely worn negligee across the chair in the corner and turned around.

Sutton had followed her into her bedroom as she'd hoped. He stood just inside the doorway, clutching the glasses in an attempt to keep control. She was surprised he hadn't snapped the delicate stems in half by now.

Lauren stalked across the room toward him, completely naked. She stopped just in front of him and reached past the glasses to the button of his collar. Her nimble fingers made quick work of his dress shirt, moving down the front until she could part the linen and place her palms on the hard, bare muscles of his chest.

He stood stone-still, his eyes partly closed as she touched him. It was all he could do with his hands still holding their drinks. He reopened them at last when she took one of the glasses from him and held it up for a toast.

"To The Eatery," she said.

"To The Eatery," Sutton repeated, his voice low and strained. He didn't drink; he just watched Lauren as she put the champagne to her lips and took a healthy sip.

"Mmm..." she said, her eyes focused only on him. "This is some really lovely stuff you've chosen for the occasion. I know what would make it better, though."

Leaning into Sutton, she held up her flute and poured a stream of the champagne down his neck. Moving quickly, she lapped at the drops that ran down his throat and pooled in the hollow of his collarbone. She let her tongue drag along his neck, meeting the rough stubble of his five o'clock shadow and feeling the low growl vibrating in his throat.

"Did you like that?" she asked.

Sutton's arm shot out to wrap around her bare waist and tug her body close. Startled, Lauren smacked hard against the wall of his chest, pressing her breasts into him. She could feel the cool moisture of the remaining champagne on his skin as it molded to hers. When she looked up, he had a wicked grin across his face.

"Oh, yeah," he said. He took a sip from his own flute and then brought his lips to hers. The bubbly liquid filled her own mouth and danced around her tongue before she swallowed it.

Their mouths were still locked onto one another as Sutton walked her slowly back toward the bed. With his arm still hooked around the small of her back, he eased Lauren's body down slowly until she met with the cool fabric of her duvet.

He pulled away long enough to look longingly at her body and whip off his shirt. Then he poured the rest of the champagne into the valley between her breasts. He cast the empty flute onto the soft carpet with a thud and dipped his head to clean up the mess he'd made. His tongue slid along her sternum, teasing at the inner curves of her breasts and down to her rib cage. He used his fingertip to dip into her navel and then rub the champagne he found there over the hardened peaks of her nipples. After bathing them in the expensive alcohol, he took his time removing every drop from her skin.

Lauren arched into his mouth and his hands, urging him on and gasping aloud as he sucked hard at her breast. Her own empty champagne flute rolled from her hand across the mattress. She brought her hands to his head, burying her fingers in his thick blond hair and tugging him closer. He resisted her pull, moving lower down her stomach to the dripping golden liquid that awaited him there. His searing lips were like fire across her skin. She ached for him to caress every part of her and he happily complied.

Sutton's hands pressed against her inner thighs, easing them apart and slipping between them and out of her reach. She cried out loudly as his champagne-chilled tongue found her heated core. His mouth worked slowly over her sensitive skin, drawing a chorus of strangled cries from her throat at the sharp contrast of sensation. He was relentless, slipping a finger inside of her and stroking until she came undone.

"Sutton!" she gasped, her body undulating and pulsing with the pleasure surging through her. She hadn't wanted to find her release without him, not tonight, but as usual, he didn't give her the option. She collapsed back against the mattress when it was over, her muscles tired and her lungs burning.

She pried open her eyes when she felt the heat of Sutton's body moving up over her again. He had shed the last of his clothing, his skin gliding bare along hers.

A moment later, his green eyes were staring down into her own and she felt herself getting lost in their emerald depths. She could feel the firm heat of his desire pressing against her thigh and her body ached to join with his. Lauren reached out to him, her palms making contact with the rough stubble of his cheeks. She pulled his mouth to hers and gave herself over to him. Not just physically, but emotionally, as well. He had believed in her, even when she hadn't believed in herself, and she wanted to be that woman for him.

At first, she'd been afraid to give in to her building feelings for Sutton. She worried that she wasn't good enough, but now, when he looked at her like this she realized it was only her own doubts holding her back. He had never said she was anything less than perfection in his eyes and she needed to stop fighting it. Stop fighting *him*. He deserved all of her, not just the woman so afraid of being a misfit that she never tried.

When he surged forward and filled her aching body with his, she gasped against his mouth but refused to let go. She needed this, needed him to have the strength to be her best self. Lauren drew her legs up to cradle his hips, urging him deeper inside. She wanted to get as close to him as she could. To take in Sutton and keep a part of him there inside her forever.

As the pace increased, Sutton finally had to tear away from her lips. He buried his face in her neck, his breath hot and ragged as he thrust hard and fast. Her body, which had been exhausted mere moments ago, was alive and tingling with sensation once again. Her release built inside, her muscles tightening and straining as she got closer and closer. Sutton's body was equally tense beneath her fingertips, a sheen of perspiration forming on his skin.

"I've never…wanted a woman…as much as I want you right now, Lauren."

His words were barely a whisper in her ear amongst the rough gasps and rustling sheets, but she heard them and felt them to her innermost core. Her heart stuttered in her chest. It wasn't a declaration of love, but it was a serious statement for a man with a playboy's reputation like his. She knew he meant it.

"I'm yours," she whispered. "I've been yours since I saw you across the room at the club."

And Lauren meant her words, as well. She wanted to say more. To pour out the sentiments that were swelling inside her chest every time she looked at him, but she wouldn't. Not now. Things in their lives were too complicated right now. And in some ways, too fragile. She was about to start a new business venture with crushing pressure to succeed. He was fighting to clear his family's name and get his company back. Any upset, like an unexpected and ill-timed declaration of love, might be enough to send the house of cards tumbling down.

The thought was sobering, but before she could get very far with her dark thoughts, her body tugged her out of her own head. The band snapped inside and the rush of pleasure exploded through her. She gasped and cried into his shoulder, clutching him tightly even as he kept surging forward again and again.

"Lauren," he rasped as his whole body shuddered with his own release.

With Sutton's face still buried in her neck and their hearts beating a rapid tattoo together, she swallowed the words on the tip of her tongue. Maybe when things settled down in their lives, they would have room for more than what they currently shared.

But not now.

Sutton rolled onto his side and wrapped his arm around her waist. He tugged her body against his, curling her into the protective cocoon to keep her warm.

"Congratulations, Chef Roberts," he whispered into her ear as she drifted into sleep.

"I was thinking we should go to the club to celebrate your big news."

Lauren opened one eye and looked at him, obviously not quite ready to be fully awake, despite the sunlight streaming into the windows. They'd been snuggling together, avoiding getting up, when he'd made the suggestion.

"Why would I want to go there?"

Sutton was a little flummoxed by her response. Most people jumped at the opportunity to visit the exclusive Royal location. "Um, well, we've run out of places to go in town. At least until that amazing new restaurant of Chef Roberts opens downtown. Why not go to the club?"

She sighed and rolled toward him, resting her head on his chest. "Let's just say it isn't my favorite place in the world. I'd basically rather go to a drive-thru to celebrate than to step foot in the Texas Cattleman's Club again."

He wrapped his arm around her, ignoring her morning grumpiness. "Remind me. We met there, didn't we? Am I remembering it wrong?"

"Yes," she replied with a tone obviously unamused with his question. "But that was different. I won the contest and Amy made me go, otherwise I wouldn't have done it. I hadn't stepped foot in that club in years."

Lauren had made several curious comments about the club, but never elaborated on why she had such negative feelings about the place. Today, he wasn't going to let her squirm out of the discussion. "Why?"

"It's just not my kind of place," she said.

"Nope. Try again."

She tried to pull away, but he held her tighter. She squirmed for a moment, and then eventually relented with a heavy sigh. "I don't like to talk about it."

"Do you think I like talking about what's going on with my family? It can't be more embarrassing than what I'm going through."

"You wanna bet?"

"Just tell me, Lauren. I need to know. Don't keep

something like this a secret from me. I need to understand what happened. You seem to hate the club and everything about it. I'm a member, so it makes me worry that in your mind I'm lumped in with the rest of it."

He felt her relax in his arms, although surrender was probably a better term for it. "Fine. So, you're a few years older, so you didn't go to the high school when I was there. If you had, you would've heard this story for sure. But anyway, I'd never been to the club before. My parents just got by, so while we might have been middle class anywhere else, we were basically poor in Royal. So suffice to say, I wasn't popular throughout school. Amy was one of my only friends, and we got through the hell of junior high and high school together."

Sutton lay silently holding her, waiting for the rest of the story. He knew it wouldn't be good, and his heart already ached for the teenage Lauren, struggling to fit in. He'd never had that problem. He and Sebastian had always been at the top of the food chain in school. He had a great time, but he also never really gave any thought to the people at Royal High that weren't enjoying their teen years. He worried that perhaps he had even made it worse for some of them, even without meaning to.

"Like most teenage girls, I had a crush on the most unobtainable guy in school. His name was Jesse. Jesse Wilde. We had chemistry class together junior year and I thought he was the most handsome guy I'd ever seen in my life. And he was nice to me. He was assigned to be my lab partner and sometimes we'd work on our chemistry homework together." She sighed. "I knew I didn't stand a chance with him—he was on the varsity basketball team and was dating the cheerleader that made my daily life hell—but I felt *seen* for the first time in a long time when I was with him."

Sutton noticed a sinking feeling start to swirl in his gut. He knew Jesse Wilde before he left Royal to go off wherever he ended up. He was young, handsome, cocky and, frankly, kind of a dick. Sutton never really had anything to do with him, but he did run into him at the club from time to time. This story wouldn't end well and part of him wanted to stop her from telling him any more. But he held his tongue.

"Our senior year came around and we ended up in the same English class. He ended up sitting behind me and would lean up and talk with me every now and then. Just enough to make my heart flutter when I felt his breath on my neck and imagined if he were to kiss me there, too. It was a stupid infatuation, but I couldn't shake it while he was still around me, making me think that I stood a chance somehow.

"About a week before the homecoming dance that year, a pipe burst in the gymnasium and it flooded over the weekend. They had to rip up all the floors and couldn't have the dance there the way they'd planned, so someone volunteered the Texas Cattleman's Club. I wasn't going, so I didn't care, but it was exciting for those who weren't members to have the chance to visit, like you'd said. Then Jesse broke up with his girlfriend a few days before the dance. It was a huge news story around the halls, with everyone speculating as to what happened and if he was into another girl."

She shook her head. "I never dreamed it would be me, but that Friday in English class, Jesse asked me to stay back after it was over because he wanted to talk to me about something. I thought he needed help with our homework on Hamlet, but it turned out that he wanted to ask me to go to homecoming with him."

Lauren sat silent for a moment before she continued. "I was over the moon. I barely slept that night. My mom even took me to Dallas that next morning to get me a dress at the last minute. My crush had asked me to homecoming and I thought everything in my life was going to change for the better." A pained expression crossed her face. "I was such a dumb, young girl. Naïve to the core. I'd never even kissed a guy before, but I thought I knew how it was all going to play out."

She chuckled bitterly. "Everything started out just the way I'd hoped. Jesse picked me up in his sweet new truck and bought me a white rose corsage for my wrist. He looked so handsome in his suit I wanted to just die. We drove to the club and went inside. Everyone was stunned to see the two of us there together. Especially his ex-girlfriend, Kaylah, who was there with some other guy I didn't know." She cleared her throat. "I didn't pay much attention to any of that, though, because I was just starstruck by the whole place. I'd always dreamed of seeing the inside and here I was, with the boy I thought I loved with every adolescent breath I took.

"So Jesse went to get us some punch and I went into the ladies' room to check my hair. I was so nervous about messing up my hair or makeup and him changing his mind because I looked bad. And when I was in there, I ran into Kaylah and a few of her friends. I expected the worst. Like I said, Kaylah seemed to take pleasure in torturing me for some reason and I figured since I was there with her ex, she had even more motivation to rip my hair out or something… But they were super nice to me. They complimented my dress and asked what I thought of the club so far."

Sutton bit back a hiss as he sucked in a wary breath. He knew girls like Kaylah and they were never suddenly nice to a girl they'd picked on without a reason. Usually a catty, awful reason.

"I thought that maybe because I was dating Jesse, I was being accepted by the popular-girl clique at last. Kaylah even offered to take me on a tour of the club since it was my first time. She managed to get me to let my guard down completely. We went into a couple different rooms and then she told me that this next one would be my favorite of them all. She opened the door and told me to go on in. It was completely dark, but I could tell the room was huge from the echoes of their voices.

"The next thing I know, I get shoved hard from behind and go flying forward. To my shock, instead of falling to the ground, I hit water. Deep water. I fought in the dark back to the surface, only to catch my breath in time for the lights to turn on and see the entire school standing around the edge of the pool laughing at me. Taking pictures on their phones. Including Jesse."

Lauren shook her head, the line of frustration deepening between her eyebrows. "He was in on it, too. He never liked me, it was just a rouse to get me to the club. I wanted to die, I was so embarrassed. I was soaked head to toe, my dress was destroyed. My hair was dripping and my makeup was melting down my face."

"What did you do?" Sutton finally spoke up, his hands curled into fists with no one to hit. He secretly hoped that Lauren could climb from the pool and punch Kaylah in the nose. But he knew that's not how these kind of stories ended. The rich, entitled Kaylahs and Jesses of the world—people he considered his friends in the past—rarely got what was coming to them.

"I did the only thing I could do. I hauled myself out of the pool while everyone laughed. And I just kept walking. I walked all the way home, dripping wet. The next day, I found out that Kaylah was jealous of Jesse talking to me so much, even though he was basically using me to pass English and not get kicked off the ball team for academic suspension. When she found out I had the audacity to have a crush on him, too, she came up with the whole idea. She convinced him to fake a breakup before the dance so he could ask me to go and she could exact her revenge. While they took me around the club on a fake tour, everyone at the dance snuck into the indoor pool room and waited for her to lure me in and push me into the pool.

"I didn't know how I would ever face going to school again. The other kids certainly didn't make it easy. But I made it through, then left immediately for culinary school in the hopes that everyone would forget about Dunk Tank."

"Dunk Tank?" Sutton perked up.

"That's what everyone called me for the rest of the school year."

"Wow," Sutton said after taking a moment to absorb the whole, horrible story. A lot of the things he'd noticed about Lauren started to make sense now. "I hate that you went through all that. Kids are incredibly cruel sometimes. I wish I had been around to kick Jesse's ass for you."

"You wouldn't have given me a second glance back then, much less come to my defense. But that's okay. Things change."

She was right. Things did change. And he couldn't let her carry this embarrassment with her forever. She was grown and successful now and none of that adolescent crap mattered anymore.

"If I were you, I wouldn't want to go back to the site of my most humiliating moment. But at the same time, I think you need to do it. Face your demons head-on, Lauren. It won't be the horrible place and people you've imagined all these years. It was the teenagers, not the club, that were the problem. They would've done something different and equally embarrassing to you in the gym if it hadn't flooded."

"Yeah, but the ringleaders were all club members."

"True. But that doesn't mean they're the awful people you remember. Like I said, teenagers are terrible. They're basically brain-damaged at that age. It's a scientific fact."

"Shush," Lauren warned, playfully swatting at his chest. "You're just making stuff up to make me feel better."

"No, it's true. Google it. Human brains aren't fully developed or matured until they're about twenty-five. So anything stupid you've done prior to that age can be blamed on underdeveloped gray matter."

"Like crushing on a guy who was a total jerk? Falling for their prank like a naïve fool and ruining my new dress? Having the whole school laugh, post embarrassing photos of me on the internet and call me Dunk Tank for the rest of my senior year?"

Sutton winced at her words. "Teenagers make bad choices all around. We all did. And now that you're older, you probably have made better choices. Including in the romance department." He smiled widely and she shook her head.

"I would say that's definitely true."

"Well, after hearing all of this, I'm sorry for the way some of the stupid people in this town have treated you. Despite not being involved, I apologize on behalf of the club and its members. I have enjoyed that indoor pool during many a cold winter here in Texas and I hate that it was the scene of one of your worst moments. Hopefully you can go back to the club and create some positive memories. Or *more* positive memories than the ones we've already made," he said with a grin. "Although I have to say, hearing this story, I'm glad you didn't punch me in the face when I led you down that dark hallway into the billiard room."

"Thankfully you said billiard, not just the pool room, or I may not have gone inside with you. And it was a different hallway, anyhow. I recognized that much. Being back in the club again, I was on high alert and I wasn't falling for that prank twice. My dress was a lot more expensive this time, so I wasn't about to ruin it."

Sutton nodded and pulled her tight against him. "So what do you say? Just one drink this afternoon to celebrate and face down your demons?"

Lauren sighed, but he felt her nod against his bare chest. "Okay. One drink."

Eleven

"You can do this. You did it the night we met and you can do it again."

Lauren took a deep breath and looked into Sutton's encouraging eyes. "I was in a mask," she muttered, but followed him inside anyway.

"It's just a drink. One drink. And if you're uncomfortable after we're done, then we'll go. But I think you'll find that what you're worried about is just a shadow of the past. The club itself is nothing more than a rustic hangout for rich cowboys."

She hoped he was right. Even so, she could feel her stomach churning as they went inside. When it wasn't done up for a party, the club had a very different feel to it. The music playing in the background was low with a country twang and the late afternoon light poured in the large windows. It gave a warm glow to the oakwood paneling on the walls and floor and highlighted the stacked stonework around the fireplace. As her first daytime visit, she now noticed the details that the dim party lighting of the night hid away, like the deer trophies and old photos of past club members that dotted the walls.

There weren't scores of people around today, but there were a few. Most of them were sitting around the bar, enjoying an early beer and a good view of the football game on the television. Others were seated at one of the tables in the dining room, eating. Off in a corner seating area, maybe even the one she'd been hiding in when she met Sutton, a couple men in Stetsons were gathered around chatting about something. They turned to give Lauren and Sutton a cursory glance as they came in, and then they returned to what they were doing.

It was very different from what she remembered. And yet her eyes went instantly to the dark hallway that lead to the club exercise facility, locker rooms and, of course, the indoor pool room. She turned instead to the other hallway that lead to the billiard room and much happier memories.

"Do you want to sit at the bar or at a private table?" Sutton asked.

"I don't care."

He didn't seem to believe her. "I'll get us a table. Less pressure to talk to strangers."

A hostess took them to a table for two by a window. Outside, she could see the tennis courts and the large Olympic-size pool that spread out beyond it. There were a few people playing tennis doubles, but no one was in the pool with the cooler weather.

She turned away from the water and focused on Sutton across the table from her. He was the only thing that mattered right now. He was here to support her. To celebrate her. To help her face the demons of her past. For his efforts, she would gladly follow him anywhere, even to the club. Especially when he sat across the table from her looking like the tastiest dish she'd ever had in her mouth.

The waiter approached, bringing them both glasses of water. "Welcome back to the club, Mr. Wingate. What can I get you and your guest today?"

"We'll have a Manhattan for me and...an extra dirty martini for the lady." He smiled, no doubt remembering the first time he'd ordered her favorite drink.

The server nodded and disappeared to retrieve their drinks from the bar.

"I hope you don't mind me ordering for you," he said. "Did I get it right?"

"You did. I would've corrected you if not."

Sutton smiled suggestively. "I'll never forget that my lady likes it extra dirty."

The server returned a moment later with their drinks and Sutton raised his glass to her. "I'd like to propose a toast, although this one will have to end differently than the last," he drawled.

Lauren raised her own cocktail to join him.

"To the most talented chef I've ever met and her new, amazingly successful restaurant!"

She smiled and clinked her martini glass against his before taking a sip. "Thank you. I appreciate how much faith you have in me. I still can't believe it's happening. But I deposited Gracie's check this morning and it cleared, so I guess I can stop pinching myself. I've never had that many zeroes in my business account before. Or my personal account. Or *ever*."

Sutton matched her smile. "It's nice, isn't it? You'd better get used to it, though. I think your success is inevitable. Before long you'll have that much and more in your account all the time. You'll have plenty of staff to help you, and things will be easier. You'll even be able to sell the food trucks and just focus on becoming the greatest chef in central Texas."

Lauren stiffened slightly in her chair and took a large sip of her martini to disguise it. He mentioned it *again*. Selling the food trucks. They really did seem to bother him. She wondered how he would respond to finding out a sale sign wasn't going up any time soon. She wanted to share her feelings with him, but not when she felt so insecure in their relationship. Not when she felt like he was constantly grooming her to be better and more successful.

"I may be able to hire some more staff and keep the trucks running. They're fairly low overhead and do pretty good business. If nothing else, having them out at lunchtime and weekend evenings would be good advertisement for the restaurant."

She expected him to react to her words, but instead he seemed to be focused on a group of men that had just come in the front door. They were chatting amongst themselves, but then they saw the two of them by the window. One nudged the other in the ribs and said something Lauren couldn't hear. The three men laughed and went off in the other direction.

When she turned back to Sutton, it looked as though the blood had drained from his face. His easy smile had faded and he looked almost rattled for the first time since she'd known him. "What's the matter? Who were those people?"

His jaw tightened and he shook his head. "They used to be friends of the family."

"And now?" she asked.

"And now they're not. Everyone wants to be your friend when you're at the top. But when you get knocked to the ground…that's when you find out who your friends really are. Those guys turned on

Sebastian and me at the first opportunity. They almost seem to enjoy our suffering. Sick bastards."

Lauren winced at his words. She supposed she was lucky to never have been in a position to have the kind of friends that used her up and left her when she was no good to them any longer. All she ever had to offer was friendship and the occasional home-cooked meal.

"I'm sorry, Sutton. At least you finally got to see their true colors."

"Yeah," he said, but she could tell his mind was far-off in thought.

"Sutton?"

He snapped his attention back to Lauren. "Would you excuse me for a moment? I'm going to run to the men's room. Will you be okay alone?"

She wanted to say no, she wouldn't be okay, but if he needed a minute to compose himself, she wouldn't deny him that. "I'll be fine. Go ahead."

He nodded and finished off the rest of his drink before pushing back his chair and heading back toward the restroom. She watched him go, noticing that more than a few of the club patrons whispered to each other as he went by. She was beginning to think maybe she was right about the club and he was wrong. The people didn't seem very friendly at all. At least not when your back was turned.

"*Dunk Tank?* Is that you?"

Lauren's blood went icy cold in her veins at the

mention of that horrid childhood nickname. She slowly turned in her seat toward the sound of a familiar woman's voice. Just behind her, to the right, a couple women were sitting together at a nearby table.

She knew instantly which one of them had spoken. She was older and a little heavier with a shiny, Botox forehead, but Lauren would've known Kaylah anywhere. She wouldn't soon forget the face of her tormentor, or the sound of her laughter as it mingled and echoed in the pool room with all the others.

Regrets flooded her mind instantly. She shouldn't have turned at the sound of that stupid nickname. She should've worn a nicer outfit. Did more with her hair or her makeup before she came to a place like this. Sutton didn't seem to care, but those sorts of things were like a woman's armor sometimes, deflecting arrows fired by her enemies.

And Kaylah Anderson was definitely her enemy. Time hadn't changed that one iota despite what Sutton seemed to think.

Lauren opted not to respond, but looked blankly at the woman. She didn't want her to think she'd made as large of an impact on her as she had. "I'm sorry, were you speaking to me?" she asked.

"Yes. You're Lauren Roberts, aren't you?"

She was surprised Kaylah knew her actual name

Lauren had never heard her say it aloud before. “Yes. Do I know you?”

“Of course, you do. I’m Kaylah Anderson-Tate. We went to high school together.” There was something wicked about the woman’s grin as she spoke. Like she was waiting for Lauren’s painful revelation so she could relive her glory.

She wasn’t going to give her that satisfaction. “I’m sorry, I don’t remember much about high school, it was so long ago.”

Kaylah frowned as well as she could without moving most of her face. “You and I had a little tiff over Jesse Wilde back in the day. Our senior year? I’m sure you recall that.”

She seemed determined for Lauren to remember her evil prank. Lauren wouldn’t bite. “Jesse Wilde. I haven’t given him a thought in ages.”

“I imagine you haven’t. Why should you when you’re on the arm of a Wingate? That’s quite the upgrade, especially for someone like you.”

The other two women tittered softly at Kaylah’s dig.

“He has good taste,” Lauren replied flatly.

“Does he, now?” She arched her eyebrows just barely in surprise. Then she leaned in and spoke in a low tone to Lauren. “Between us girls, how did you happen to snag Sutton Wingate? He’s always been known for being so...*particular*.”

Lauren didn’t respond. What was she going to

say to that? During her time with Sutton, she'd come to learn he had a bit of a playboy past. Playboys tended to be drawn to the beautiful and elegant type of women. She wasn't sure she would use either of those words to describe herself. She was attractive enough, but glamorous? Not with her hair in a bun, no makeup and a chef's jacket covered in juices from butchering a large chunk of meat for dinner service.

She might have fit the bill that first night with her gown, mask and bold alter ego working for her, but not now. Maybe encouraging her to sell the trucks was Sutton's way of nudging her one step closer to the beautiful and glamorous woman he truly wanted.

"Keeping your secrets, eh?" Kaylah replied to her silence with a pointed chuckle. "Ah, well, I guess it doesn't really matter. Sutton never keeps a lady around for long. Whatever you did might've worked to lure him in, but it won't keep him around forever. I wouldn't get too attached."

The other women laughed again and Lauren forced herself to turn back to her table. She wished Sutton hadn't left. She'd been alone and exposed when the worst possible person could've shown up. If he'd been here, maybe he would've stood up for her and shut Kaylah down. Or said something that would prop up her crumbling ego when she needed it the most.

But alone, she was falling apart. Somehow Kaylah had been able to speak to her darkest fears without even trying. Lauren already knew she loved a man she had a tentative hold on, at best. But having her point it out as though it were so obvious was that much more painful.

Lauren didn't want to be at the club a moment longer. She didn't want to be around such fickle and catty people for any more time than she had to be. And if Sutton couldn't see these folks for who they really were, then maybe it was because he belonged here with them.

But she certainly didn't. And never would. And as painful as it was to admit, perhaps she needed to stop seeing Sutton. Dating him was overreaching from her station in town.

Lauren picked up her clutch and got up without another word. She was taking her dignity and her food trucks and she was going home.

Coming to the club was a mistake. Sutton knew that now. He just hadn't realized that it would be *his* reputation, and not Lauren's, that caused the problems.

He'd been deliberately avoiding the club these last few weeks. While he knew that people, including the ones who'd recently claimed to be friends, were talking about his family behind their backs, avoiding the club made it easier to ignore. Beth's charity event had been the exception. But the distraction of Lauren and helping with her restaurant had proved too successful. In encouraging her to face her fears, he'd forgotten why *he* hadn't wanted to come.

Less than two sips into his cocktail, he had remembered. He'd felt the eyes on them when they came in, but chalked it up to Lauren being new. But when the others started laughing and he'd picked up enough of their words to know the joke was on him, he knew he'd made an error in coming here.

He splashed his face with water at the sink and took a deep breath. He needed to get it together. He couldn't let them know they were getting to him. That was paramount. Sutton and his family had nothing to hide. They'd been set up. All those fair-weather friends could enjoy their laugh at his expense, but in the end, the truth would come out. And when they tried to cozy back up to the Wingates in the future, they'd find an icy reception.

Plucking a towel from the dispenser, Sutton dried his face and hands and used a splash of the complimentary cologne he liked to pat on his neck. It had eucalyptus, which was supposed to be good for stress. He could use all the help he could get at the moment.

When he returned to the dining room, he thought for a moment that he'd gotten himself turned around. But he knew he was at the right table. Their two empty drink glasses—one martini glass and one lowball—were still sitting there. But Lauren was nowhere to be seen.

"Will that be all for you, Mr. Wingate?" the waiter asked as he approached.

"I don't know. I think so. Did you see where the lady that was with me went?"

"No sir. She must've slipped away when I was in the kitchen. Would you like me to add the bill to your membership tab?"

Sutton nodded. "Yes, thank you." He doubted she would want to stay on at the club past the single drink she agreed to, even if she'd only gone to the ladies' room or stepped out to use her phone. He certainly didn't want to stay. But where had she gone? Lauren hadn't vanished on him since their first night together at the club.

"She left. Ordered a car to pick her up, I think."

Sutton turned toward a group of women sitting nearby and the one that had spoken to him. "She left the club?"

"Yes. A few minutes ago. She seemed pretty upset, too."

He narrowed his gaze at the unfamiliar brunette. She seemed pleased and perhaps all too eager to tell him what happened. He had no clue who she was or why that would be the case. Ignoring her, he rushed over to the front door and flung it open to see if he still had time to catch her.

He saw her standing on the curb as a white sedan with an Uber sticker in the front window pulled up to her. "Lauren!" he shouted as he ran down the stairs to her.

She didn't turn his way, instead scrambling to get into the car before he could reach her. He was able to reach out and grasp her wrist, tugging her back to her feet.

"What's going on?" Sutton implored. "Why are you leaving?"

Lauren looked up at him with eyes near overflowing with tears. He could see hurt and conflict dancing across her face. She opened her mouth to say something, then shook her head. Leaning in to Sutton, she pressed a heated kiss to his lips. There was a finality in the way she touched him, and it made his chest ache.

"You need to let me go," she whispered against his mouth and pulled her wrist from his grasp.

Sutton stood, confused and heartbroken, as Lauren got into the car and it drove away. He watched the Uber disappear down the highway and wondered what the hell had just happened.

Picking his phone from his coat pocket, he dialed Lauren, but it went immediately to voicemail. He didn't understand how things had soured so quickly.

The sound of those same men laughing in the far corner of the room caught his attention as he hung up and stepped back into the club's lobby. "I hope he looks good in orange!" one of them said to another loud round of laughter.

They were belittling him and his family again. They didn't even try to pretend like they weren't. He was used to it, even before the scandal people were always talking about his family. But it was new to Lauren. Maybe she'd overheard their ugly jokes while he was away from the table. He'd told her everything there was to know about the situation with Wingate Industries, but perhaps being here and having to face his scandal head-on was too much for her. It was one thing to say he was being investigated and plead his innocence. It was quite another to hear men joke about the man she was dating going to federal prison. Who wanted to carry on a relationship that might consist of Sunday afternoon visits through Plexiglas and parole hearings?

His declaration of innocence didn't mean he wouldn't end up in prison anyway. He wasn't that naïve. They had good lawyers, *expensive* lawyers, but whoever had set them up had done a thorough job. With the evidence they had and the right jury, Sutton, Sebastian and countless other executives at the company could spend the next year or so behind bars.

The idea bothered him, of course. No one wanted to go to prison. But now the thought of it really ate at him knowing he would have to leave Lauren to build her new restaurant without his help and support.

All of that was a lot to process and might be hard for her to face. And more trouble than she needed right now in her busy life. He didn't blame her for running, if that was what she'd done. She was an up-and-coming star in Royal, whether she knew it or not. She didn't need Sutton's drama dragging her down and tarnishing her reputation before she'd had a chance to build one.

That didn't mean it wasn't a punch to the gut he wasn't expecting. He didn't think she was the kind of woman to run out when things got tough.

Without glancing back at the men he'd once called friends, Sutton let the door swing shut behind him and walked to his car. He drove back to his rental house faster than he should've, inviting more trouble with the law, but he didn't care. He just wanted away from the club. Away from those people he'd defended to Lauren, but now, wondered why. Perhaps she was right to avoid them all. He might need to take a page from her book and let his own membership lapse for a while. It was one less expense piling up with the others.

Once back in the safety of the house, where he could stick his head in the sand and ignore the troubles he'd had to face today, he threw his keys down on the kitchen counter. Sutton pulled a beer from the fridge and popped off the top with enough angry force to send the metal disk flying through the air.

It landed at his brother's feet.

"You're back early," Sebastian said as he came around the corner into the kitchen and looked down at the silver disk on the tile. He stopped short when he looked at Sutton, the beer in his hand and the scowl on his face. "Uh-oh. What happened?"

Sutton relayed his experience at the club as briefly as he could. "She ran out on me."

"Did you try calling her?"

He pulled out his phone and dialed again, only to have Lauren's voice mail announcement tell him to leave a message. Again. "She's not taking my calls at the moment."

"I wonder what happened while you were in the restroom." Sebastian settled into a barstool with a thoughtful expression on his face. "Whatever it was, it happened fast."

"It's got to be about the investigation. The Kennedy brothers and Mark Swenson were being jackasses about it when we were there. Joking about us in orange jumpsuits." He shook his head. "As much as I hate to say it, it was probably best that she left. I would've bailed if I was her. No one wants to be in a relationship with a criminal if they can avoid it. Maybe she decided to make a run for it while she still had the chance. Things haven't gotten too serious yet."

"For one thing, you're not a criminal and I'd like to think Lauren knows that. For another, if you think things aren't too serious, you're blind."

Sutton swallowed his sip of beer and set the bottle down on the granite countertop. "What are you talking about?"

Sebastian rolled his eyes. "Really? You don't think that what you two have going isn't serious? It's the most serious relationship I've seen you in, Sutton. Like, *ever*. You've fallen hard for that woman, whether you've admitted it to yourself or not."

He opened his mouth to argue, but stopped short. The more he thought about his brother's words, the more he realized that they were right. Sutton had never had feelings for a woman like he had for Lauren. She hadn't just been a distraction from his problems. She had become the reason he had to fight through them and come out the other side stronger. She was the first thing he thought of when he woke up in the morning and the last thing on his mind as he drifted off to sleep. When he wasn't with her, he felt like there was a hole in his gut and no amount of antacids could fix it. Only holding her in his arms again did the trick.

And it wasn't just about sex, for once. Relationships with him had always centered around physical gratification and having fun. And when he grew bored with either, he moved on. It was completely different with her. Sex with Lauren was mind-blowing, no doubt, but he was also content to just snuggle with her on the couch. He liked to draw the scent of her shampoo into his lungs and try to memorize it. He felt like the world was instantly better when he saw her smile.

There was no longer any doubt in his mind. He hated to admit it, but Sebastian was right. He was in love with Lauren. She just had to bail on him to reveal the truth of it.

And now that he knew, he just had to figure out what he was going to do about his runaway lover.

Twelve

Lauren wasn't quite sure how to handle her new normal. In order to get the restaurant up and running, she had to relinquish control of other things. That meant not spending every waking moment dealing with the food trucks. Ed and Javier still ran the second truck, but she'd hired someone to help Amy work the first truck. She developed the daily menus a week in advance and let Amy and Javier handle the details.

It was a big step for her, but in order to keep everyone gainfully employed and funds coming in, the trucks had to keep going for now. Especially with business booming after the exposure of the pop-up night. Once the restaurant was open, perhaps she could keep hiring on folks to run the trucks and move her main crew to the kitchen. They knew her food better than anyone and she would need their support to make it a success.

But that was a decision for later. Right now, she had plenty of things to think about that had to be dealt with immediately. She'd already signed the lease on the restaurant space, so every day that went by without them making money, the more nervous she became. That meant she had to move quickly on choosing contractors for repairs, paint, carpet and more. Things she wanted to focus on—namely the menu—had to take second place to all the environmental decisions.

Thankfully, she had Gracie to help. The new millionaire and investor wasn't quite as silent a partner as Lauren had expected, but it had turned out for the best. Gracie wanted to help with as much as she could, so Lauren was turning over a few decisions on the decor and furnishings to her. So far, she'd chosen flatware, plates and even the new fixtures in the restrooms. Furniture was on order. That took a few worries off Lauren's plate.

It actually took enough off her mind that she found her thoughts straying periodically. Normally, she was too busy to think much about her life and how it was going. But now that she had a little time, her brain seemed all too happy to put aside menu ideas and circle back to thinking about Sutton and the look on his face as she drove away. About how much she missed him. And how she'd run out on him without explaining why or what happened.

With a sigh, Lauren dropped her pen back onto the counter and sat back. Thoughts of shrimp and grits went to the wayside as she glanced over at her phone. She had six missed calls. All from Sutton, although they were coming less frequently now. Soon he would stop calling entirely, a reality that both relieved and terrified her.

She needed to explain herself. To explain to him why she ran off. But it seemed stupid every time she tried to come up with an answer. The truth was ugly and hard to explain. How do you get the town golden boy, the millionaire playboy tycoon, to understand that she had low self-esteem? He wouldn't understand. And yet, he'd contributed to it, likely without even knowing what he was really doing.

Lauren already spent most of her time feeling insecure. His constant suggestions about her business, coupled with running into Kaylah at the club of all places, was just too much. She didn't feel good enough for this town most days, but that afternoon she'd gotten confirmation that she was right. She was a great chef and could happily serve the elite of Royal amazing food, but she would never be one of them.

The sooner she admitted that to herself, the easier it would be in the end. She might love Sutton. And he might be infatuated with the idea of her. But he would never love her. His family and friends would never accept her. So the next time the phone rang and it was him, she would continue to ignore it. It was easier on her heart this way.

As if on cue, her phone started to play the ringtone she'd assigned to Sutton. She sighed and turned away from the phone. Instead of answering, she got up and made herself a glass of iced tea. But the moment the phone stopped ringing, her doorbell pinged loudly through the house.

Lauren frowned and made her way to the front door. She couldn't keep up with the packages showing up of late. She opened it, expecting to find a delivery man with eight cases of dinner plates, but instead found Sutton on her porch with another bouquet of herbs in his hands.

Her heart leaped as she saw him, ignoring the sinking feeling of dread in her stomach. It seems he wouldn't take no for an answer when it came to her and she loved that about him. And hated it at the same time. How was she supposed to convince herself she could move on without him in her life if he wouldn't let her try?

"What are you doing here, Sutton?" she asked in a defeated tone. She hadn't answered the phone because she wasn't ready to talk to him. Showing up on her doorstep just forced her to face the feelings and words she was too emotionally exhausted to deal with right now.

He smiled and held out the bouquet. "I'm here because I'm not sure what happened between us, but I'm determined to fix it."

"You don't have to fix it, Sutton. Or fix me. I'm supposed to be your girlfriend, not a pet project for a bored businessman trying to avoid the problems in his own life."

He looked confused and slightly stunned by her sharp words. "What are you talking about?"

She wasn't sure what he was missing from the conversation. What was he talking about? His befuddled look made her just as perplexed. She just shook her head. There wasn't time for this. "Just go home, Sutton."

"I was home," he said. "But it felt cold and empty without you there with me. Nothing feels right since you ran off and I don't know what to do about it, because I'm not sure what I did wrong. So tell me and let me do something about it, because I need you."

"You didn't do anything wrong," Lauren replied, trying not to react physically to his bold words. She felt cold and empty without him, too, but she wouldn't say so.

"Then why did you run out on me at the club?"

"Because you deserve better!" she shouted.

Sutton's jaw dropped at her forceful words. Then

his expression softened with sadness in his eyes. "There isn't anything better than you, Lauren."

Now it was her turn to be struck silent by his words. He meant it. She could feel the truth of his proclamation down to the soles of her feet. But she couldn't understand why. Everyone seemed to realize their relationship was doomed but Sutton. He was just too stubborn to see it.

"May I come in?" he asked softly.

Lauren relented and stepped back to let him inside. She took the herbs he offered and carried them into the kitchen to put the cuttings in some fresh water. They would be good for a chimichurri or pesto sauce later. Even then, a chef's brain never fully switched off.

With that settled, she ushered Sutton into her small living room and the comfortable set of chairs she had there. They sat on opposite ends of the loveseat, only inches apart, but it felt like miles to Lauren. She wanted to scoot in and find sweet solace in the nook of his arm. But she stayed in place.

"Despite what you might think, Sutton, I'm not good enough for you. I'm not the right kind of girl for your family and friends. I don't fit in with the club crowd and despite your best efforts, my trip there only reinforced what I already knew. What we've had is fun, but it isn't built to last."

Sutton's eyes narrowed as she spoke, his jaw flexing with suppressed irritation. "Where do you get off deciding that you're not good enough for me? Shouldn't I be the one to make that decision?"

"You didn't have to make it. Good old Kaylah Anderson took care of the dirty work for you. One quick conversation and the fantasy was over, with my feet instantly back on the ground. I know I'm fighting an uphill battle I'm destined to lose, now."

Sutton frowned and then his eyes met hers. "Are you talking about the brunette at the club? The one sitting near our table in a blue blouse?"

"That was her." Of course, he would notice a woman like Kaylah. Everyone noticed her, with her golden hair, big blue eyes and huge chest. And if they didn't, Kaylah was quick to make them notice her.

"What does she…?" His voice trailed off and his eyes widened as he seemed to piece it all together. "Wait. Was that woman the same Kaylah you mentioned from the homecoming dance at the club?"

She nodded. "It was a quick discussion, but one I needed to hear. I'd let things go too far between us. Overreached, just like with Jesse. I was just going to get hurt."

"And what about me getting hurt? I was already feeling down, but then you ran out on me without a word and refused to return my calls. It hurt me that you would pull away without even trying to talk to me."

Lauren scoffed. "You're Sutton Wingate. You'll

have some buxom, poised socialite on your arm in no time and you'll forget all about me and how hurt you are."

"Forget about you?" He sounded incredulous. "I can't forget about you, Lauren. Believe me, I've tried. Those days after the masquerade party, I couldn't get you out of my mind. You haunted my dreams."

"That girl wasn't me. She was glamorous and elegant and all the things I'm not. That night was a fluke and you fell for nothing more than some fancy window dressing courtesy of the *Cinderella Sweepstakes*. Take away the masks and the makeup and all you have left is me."

"Take all that away and all that's left is a smart, talented, caring, sexy woman who means more to me than anyone else. You talk about yourself as though I could ever be disappointed in who you are or how you look. I fell for you without even having seen your face. And once the mask was gone, things only got better. The real woman is so much more amazing than the mystery could ever be. And when I thought I'd driven you away by the mess my life had become, I wanted to kick myself."

"Driven away?" Lauren asked. "What do you mean?"

Sutton sighed. "When we went to the club that day, the laughter on the other side of the room was all I could hear or think about. The others joking about my family's misfortune and how we're all just criminals doomed to wind up in jail… It taunted me from almost the moment we stepped inside. I knew that going to the club was a mistake then, but it was important for me to keep it together and help you get over your fears—" regret tightened the corners of his mouth "—That's why I had to take a minute away. I was embarrassed by the talk, but didn't want you, or them, to know it. When you vanished, I thought maybe you'd heard enough and decided I wasn't worth the trouble. You would've been right if you had. Because I think you deserve better than a mess like me."

Lauren's mouth dropped open, her expression one of utter disbelief. "How could you believe you're not worth the trouble? You're an incredible man. An *innocent* man. And seeing you through these rough times is absolutely worth it."

He was relieved that she thought so, but he still felt the need to explain himself. "And when I came here today, you were right about me constantly trying to fix things. I have probably made you feel worse about yourself with my misplaced drive to succeed. You don't need fixing and I never meant to imply that you did."

"Sutton, I—"

He held up a hand. "No, please let me finish. This needs to be said." Swallowing hard, he continued. “I realize now that your business is yours to run however you want to. If you want food trucks or a restaurant or a hot dog stand, that’s your choice and I’m happy to stand by your side whatever you want to do. The truth is that I wasn’t pushing you because you weren’t good enough. I was pushing you because I felt useless. I’ve had all this power and control from the moment my brother and I took over the business from my father when he got sick. And in an instant, the bottom fell out on us all and it was stripped away.

“I had everything and suddenly, I had nothing. Choosing which coffee to make in the morning was as close as I got to making an important decision. Then I found that helping with your business made me feel useful again. I was able to help you build and grow and achieve goals that you may not have even had, but I couldn’t stop myself. I’m sorry for turning your life into a project.”

Lauren moved closer to him on the couch and reached out to place her hand over his. “Don’t apologize. You got me to dream bigger than I ever would have on my own. Because of you and your help, I’m opening my dream restaurant. Without you, Sutton, it would’ve taken me years to work up the nerve to even try. You refused to let me stand behind imaginary barriers and pushed me to be my best self—” she released a ragged breath “—Yes, I worried that you were pushing me so I was good enough for some standard society had set, but I went along with it because I wanted to be worthy of someday being a Wingate, and—"

"Wait," Sutton interrupted. His heart stuttered at the words she'd just said. "Did you just say you wanted to be a…a Wingate?"

Lauren's cheeks flushed red and her lips pressed tightly together as she tried to suppress her embarrassment. She'd obviously said more than she intended to. "I didn't mean anytime soon, obviously. There are other factors at play, of course. And we've just started, really uh…"

"I love you, Lauren."

It was the first time he'd said those words aloud to anyone aside from his close family, and even they were not a particularly touchy-feely group. He'd certainly never even come close to saying it to a woman before. The phrase felt amazing on his lips so he said it again. "I love you."

"I heard you the first time," she said with wide eyes. "I just thought perhaps I was imagining it."

Sutton leaned in and took her hand into his own. "You're not imagining anything. I love you. And I love you just as you are. I don't care if you're wearing fancy gowns, sweatpants or your chef's whites. You are perfect and I'll never try to change who you are."

Lauren sat silent and still as he spoke. After a

moment without a response, he reached out to caress her cheek. "Lauren?"

"I love you, too," she blurted out as she snapped back to life and took a deep breath of relief. "Even after you said it first, it was still a little scary to finally say the words out loud."

"You scared me for a second," Sutton admitted with a smile. He leaned in and pressed his lips to hers. He'd missed the feeling of touching her these last few days. Actually, he'd missed everything about her, but didn't want to push her if she wasn't ready to talk. Now he had her back in his arms for the second time and, this time, he wasn't letting go.

The warm sensation of love filled his chest for the first time and urged him on. He told himself before he came here today that he was going to say everything that was on his mind. If she rejected him, he would cope with that and move on, but so far, so good.

Forcing himself to break off the kiss, he sat back and looked into the golden brown eyes that had first captivated him at the party. "Lauren, I know that you have a lot on your mind with the restaurant and all. But do you think you can answer one more question for me?"

"Of course," Lauren said. "What is it?"

"I've been thinking a lot about us these last few days and about what I would say if you finally answered the phone again. I've run it over in my mind dozens of times. And the most important part is not only that I love you, but that I can't envision my future without you in it any longer. I want to be there when you open the doors of The Eatery for the first night and the hundredth night and the thousandth night. And I want you to be at my side when we walk back into the family estate with our names cleared at last."

Sutton clutched her hand and slipped off the couch onto his knee. "But most importantly, I want to spend the rest of my life with you, Lauren. Which is why I was so happy to hear you say you'd thought about becoming a Wingate. Because honestly, truly, the only thing I would ever change about you…is your last name. Will you marry me?"

Tears started welling in Lauren's eyes. Thankfully, a smile spread across her face and allayed his fears. "I will," she said. "Absolutely, yes!"

Sutton leapt to his feet and pulled Lauren up with him. He wrapped her in his arms, hugging her tightly against him before capturing her lips in a sizzling kiss. There was a time this week when he thought he might not get to hold her again. And now, he had his bride-to-be wrapped in his protective embrace.

When he could finally bear to pull away from her, he reached into his pocket and pulled out a small jewelry box. "I picked this out, but if you don't like it, we can absolutely take it back for a different design." He opened it up and held up the engagement ring he'd chosen for her. It was a bezel set, round, two karat solitaire with channel-set diamonds in the platinum band. It was beautiful, but it was even more important to him that the ring would be easy for her to wear. She was in a constant state of putting on and removing food service gloves and he didn't want it snagging or, God forbid, falling into someone's meal.

Now he just held his breath and waited for the verdict. And it came when she plucked it from the box and slipped it onto her finger, beaming with pride.

"It's perfect," she breathed. "Actually, it's beyond perfect. I never dreamed of anything as lovely as this is."

"Do you mean it? I didn't want it to interfere with your work, so I chose a setting that was mostly flat."

Lauren admired it for another moment and then caressed his cheek. "I do mean it."

"I'm glad. And I know you're busy ramping up the new restaurant, so I don't want you to worry about the wedding right now. There's no hurry. Maybe by next summer, you'll be comfortable enough to take some time away and could use the break. And if I'm lucky, maybe the Wingate Estate will be back in our hands. If so, we can have a beautiful wedding there. Or wherever you want, really. It's entirely up to you."

"All I care about is the food," Lauren said with a smile.

"I thought you might say that. It's going to be hard to find a caterer talented enough to make you happy, but I look forward to taste testing until we find one."

Lauren shook her head and looked at him with eyes full of love and excitement. She had the same expression on her face as she did when Gracie offered to invest in the restaurant. He'd been jealous that day that he hadn't been responsible for making her dreams come true. But now, as she looked at him with the same unabashed joy, he realized he'd succeeded. She had more than one dream and he was a part of them all.

"You are amazingly thoughtful, Sutton Wingate. You bring me bouquets of fragrant herbs instead of pretty, but useless flowers. You choose an engagement ring that won't snag on anything so I can wear it always. You offer to eat your way through Texas with me to find just the right caterer. Who would've expected that underneath it all the big, bad wolf was such a softie?"

"Don't tell anyone," he said with a grin. "You never know when you might need your wolf to huff and puff and blow someone's house down."

"What a big heart you have."

"The better to love you with, my dear."

Epilogue

The restaurant was really coming together.

Lauren took a step back from the accent wall they were painting bright blue and smiled. Her vision was coming to life and soon, she would have everything she ever wanted.

"I feel like a Smurf."

She turned to where Sutton was rolling the wall a few feet down. He was covered in tiny blue speckles of cast off, in addition to smears of white, red and black paint all over his clothes. They'd been painting for what felt like days, but they were in the homestretch. From there, they'd have the new hardwood floors laid and they could bring in all the new furniture Gracie had ordered.

"You make an adorable one," Lauren said as she leaned in to give him a kiss.

"That only makes me feel slightly better," Sutton returned as he laid down the paint roller.

"How about if I offer to give you a sponge bath later and make sure every drop of paint is gone by bedtime?"

His wicked grin returned. "That sounds like a plan."

Before she could respond, Sutton's cell phone starting ringing on the floor a few feet away. He turned to look at it, frowning at the screen. "It's my brother, Miles."

"Hey Miles. What's going on?"

Lauren sat the edging brush down in the paint tray and walked over to where he was standing. She couldn't hear the conversation on the line, but she could tell by the suddenly serious expression on his face that it was important.

"Okay. I'll be there." Sutton hung up the phone, continuing to frown at the blank screen.

"What is it?" Lauren asked.

"My brother says he's found out something important, but he wouldn't elaborate over the phone. He called an emergency family meeting tonight at six."

"What do you think it's about?"

Sutton shook his head. "I don't know for sure, but judging by the sound of his voice, he may have found the piece of information we've been looking for."

"What piece of information?"

Sutton sighed and rubbed his face thoughtfully. "If we're lucky…maybe the evidence we need to prove to the world that the Wingates were set up. And by whom."

* * * * *

Don't miss a single installment in
Texas Cattleman's Club: Rags to Riches!

Available June 2020 through January 2021!

The Price of Passion *by* USA TODAY
bestselling author Maureen Child

Black Sheep Heir *by* USA TODAY
bestselling author Yvonne Lindsay

The Paternity Pact *by Cat Schield*

Trust Fund Fiancé *by* USA TODAY
bestselling author Naima Simone

Billionaire Behind the Mask *by Andrea Laurence*

In Bed with His Rival *by* USA TODAY
bestselling author Katherine Garbera

Tempted by the Boss *by* USA TODAY
bestselling author Jules Bennett

One Night in Texas *by* USA TODAY
bestselling author Charlene Sands

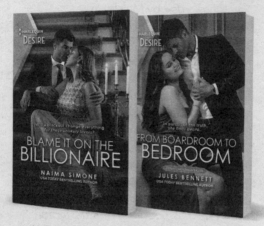

COMING NEXT MONTH FROM

HARLEQUIN

DESIRE

Available November 3, 2020

#2767 CLAIMING THE RANCHER'S HEIR

Gold Valley Vineyards • by Maisey Yates

It's Christmas and rancher Creed Cooper must work with his rival, Wren Maxfield—so tempers flare! But animosity becomes passion and, now, Wren is pregnant. Creed wants a marriage in name only. But as desire takes over, this may be a vow neither can keep...

#2768 IN BED WITH HIS RIVAL

Texas Cattleman's Club: Rags to Riches

by Katherine Garbera

With a bitter legal battle between their families, lawyer Brian Cooper knows he should stay away from Piper Holloway. For Piper, having a fling with a younger man is fun...until stunning truths are revealed. Now can she ever trust him with her heart?

#2769 SLOW BURN

Dynasties: Seven Sins • by Janice Maynard

Jake Lowell has been a globe-trotting playboy for years, ignoring all his family obligations. Until he learns his one hot night with hardworking Nikki Reardon resulted in a child. Will his history threaten a future with the woman who got away?

#2770 VOWS IN NAME ONLY

Billionaires of Boston • by Naima Simone

When CEO Cain Farrell is blackmailed into marrying his enemy's daughter, he vows it will be a marriage on paper only. But one sizzling kiss with Devon Cole changes everything. Can he look past her father's sins to build a real future together?

#2771 THE SINNER'S SECRET

Bad Billionaires • by Kira Sinclair

Wrongly convicted executive Gray Lockwood will stop at nothing to prove his innocence, including working with the woman who put him behind bars, accountant Blakely Whittaker. But now this billionaire realizes he doesn't just want justice, he wants her...

#2772 ALL HE WANTS FOR CHRISTMAS

The Sterling Wives • by Karen Booth

Andrew Sterling wants one thing: to destroy his dead brother's company. But when his brother's widow, Miranda, invites Andrew over for the holidays, attraction ignites. He'll have to choose between the woman in his bed and the resentment that has guided him until now...

YOU CAN FIND MORE INFORMATION ON UPCOMING HARLEQUIN TITLES, FREE EXCERPTS AND MORE AT HARLEQUIN.COM.

It's Christmas and rancher Creed Cooper must work with his rival, Wren Maxfield—and tempers flare! But animosity becomes passion and, now, Wren is pregnant. Creed wants a marriage in name only. But as desire takes over, this may be a vow neither can keep...

Read on for a sneak peek at
Claiming the Rancher's Heir
by New York Times *bestselling author Maisey Yates!*

"Come here," he said, his voice suddenly hard. "I want to show you something."

There was a big white tent that was still closed, reserved for an evening hors d'oeuvre session for people who had bought premium tickets, and he compelled her inside. It was already set up with tables and tablecloths, everything elegant and dainty, and exceedingly Maxfield. Though there were bottles of Cowboy Wines on each table, along with bottles of Maxfield select.

But they were not apparently here to look at the wine, or indeed anything else that was set up. Which she discovered when he cupped her chin with firm fingers and looked directly into her eyes.

"I've done nothing but think about you for two weeks. I want you. Not just something hot and quick against a wall. I need you in a bed, Wren. We need some time to explore this. To explore each other."

She blinked. She had not expected that.

He'd been avoiding her and she'd been so sure it was because he didn't want this.

But he was here in a suit.

And he had a look of intent gleaming in those green eyes.

She realized then she'd gotten it all wrong.

"I…I agree."

She also hadn't expected to agree.

"I want you now," she whispered, and before she could stop herself, she was up on her tiptoes and kissing that infuriating mouth.

She wanted to sigh with relief. She had been so angry at him. So angry at the way he had ignored this. Because how dare he? He had never ignored the anger between them. No. He had taken every opportunity to goad and prod her in anger. So why, why had he ignored this?

But he hadn't.

They were devouring each other, and neither of them cared that there were people outside. His large hands palmed her ass, pulling her up against his body so she could feel just how hard he was for her. She arched against him, gasping when the center of her need came into contact with his rampant masculinity.

She didn't understand the feelings she had for this man. Where everything about him that she found so disturbing was also the very thing that drove her into his arms.

Too big. Too rough. Crass. Untamable. He was everything she detested, everything she desired.

All that, and he was distracting her from an event that she had planned. Which was a cardinal sin in her book. And she didn't even care.

He set her away from him suddenly, breaking their kiss. "Not now," he said, his voice rough. "Tonight. All night. You. In my bed."